Hiccup Horrendous Haddock the Third was an awesome swordfighter, a dragon whisperer, and the greatest Viking Hero who ever lived. But Hiccup's memoirs look back to when he was a very ordinary boy who found it hard to be a hero.

You don't *have* to read the Hiccup memoirs in order. But if you want to, this is the right order:

WARNING

Any relationship to
any historical fact
WHATSOEVER is
entirely coincidental.

YOU HAVE BEEN
WARNED

The translator would like to dedicate this book to her brother, CASPAR, with love and admiration.

Text and illustrations copyright © 2003, 2014 by Cressida Cowell
Text and illustrations from *How to Train Your Viking* copyright © 2006 by Cressida Cowell
Text and illustrations from *The Day of the Dreader* copyright © 2012 by Cressida Cowell
Text and illustrations in excerpt from *How to Be a Pirate* copyright © 2004 by Cressida Cowell

Little, Brown and Company

Hachette Book Group
1290 Avenue of the Americas, New York, NY 10104
Visit our website at lb-kids.com

Little, Brown and Company is a division of Hachette Book Group, Inc.
The Little, Brown name and logo are trademarks of Hachette Book Group, Inc.

First U.S. Special Edition: May 2014
First U.S. Special Collector's Edition: May 2014
First U.S. Hardcover Edition published in May 2004 by Little, Brown and Company
Originally published in Great Britain in 2003 by Hodder Children's Books

A big thank you to Andrea Malaskova and Judit Komar

How to Train Your Viking originally published in Great Britain in 2006 by Hodder Children's Books.

This book is dedicated to my grandpa ALAN and my grandmas Nancy and JILL because they all told me stories.

The Day of the Dreader originally published in Great Britain in 2012 by Hodder Children's Books.

Please note... Any relationship to any historical fact WHATSOEVER is entirely coincidental.

Library of Congress Cataloging-in-Publication Data

Cowell, Cressida.
   How to train your dragon / by Hiccup Horrendous Haddock III ;
translated from the Old Norse by Cressida Cowell. — 1st U.S. ed.
    p. cm.
   Summary: Chronicles the adventures and misadventures of Hiccup Horrendous Haddock the Third as he tries to pass the important initiation test of his Viking clan, the Tribe of the Hairy Hooligans, by catching and training a dragon.
   ISBN 978-0-316-73737-1 (hc) — ISBN 978-0-316-08527-4 (pb) — ISBN 978-0-316-40747-2 (special edition) — ISBN 978-0-316-33363-4 (special collector's edition)
   1. Vikings — Juvenile fiction. [1. Vikings — Fiction. 2. Dragons — Fiction. 3. Humorous stories.] I. Title.

PZ7.C83535Ho 2004
[Fic] — dc21
                        2003054538

10 9 8 7 6 5 4 3

RRD-C

Printed in the United States of America

How to Train Your Dragon

SPECIAL EDITION

How to Train Your Dragon

The Heroic Misadventures of
Hiccup the Viking

as told to
Cressida Cowell

LITTLE, BROWN AND COMPANY
New York   Boston

~Novices of the Hairy Hooligan Tribe~

Hiccup

clueless

DOGSBREATH THE DUHBRAIN

Tuffnut Junior

Speedifist

Fishlegs

WART,HOG

Snotlout

~ CONTENTS ~

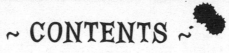

ISLE of BERK

Caliban Caves

Wild Dragon Cliff

Hooligan Village

Madman's Gully

Black Heart Bay

Highest Point

Harbor

Hooligan

HUGE HILL

The Little Isles

Cowrie Beach

Puffin Point

Hiccup
Horrendous
HADDOCK
the
Third

A Note from the Hero

There were dragons when I was a boy.

There were great, grim, sky dragons that nested on the cliff tops like gigantic scary birds. Little, brown, scuttly dragons that hunted down the mice and rats in well-organized packs. Preposterously huge Sea Dragons that were twenty times as big as the Big Blue Whale and who killed for the fun of it.

You will have to take my word for it, for the dragons are disappearing so fast they may soon become extinct.

Nobody knows what is happening. They are crawling back into the sea from whence they came, leaving not a bone, not a fang, in the earth for the men of the future to remember them by.

So, in order that these amazing creatures should not be forgotten, I will tell this true story from my childhood.

I was not the sort of boy who could train a dragon with a mere lifting of an eyebrow. I was not a natural at the Heroism business. I had to work at it. This is the story of becoming a Hero the Hard Way.

1. FIRST CATCH YOUR DRAGON

Long ago, on the wild and windy isle of Berk, a smallish Viking with a longish name stood up to his ankles in snow.

Hiccup Horrendous Haddock the Third, the Hope and Heir to the Tribe of the Hairy Hooligans, had been feeling slightly sick ever since he woke up that morning.

Ten boys, including Hiccup, were hoping to become full members of the Tribe by passing the Dragon Initiation Program. They were standing on a bleak little beach at the bleakest spot on the whole bleak island. A heavy snow was falling.

"**PAY ATTENTION!**" screamed Gobber the Belch, the soldier in charge of teaching Initiation. "This will be your first military operation, and Hiccup will be commanding the team."

"Oh, not Hic-cup," groaned Dogsbreath the Duhbrain and most of the other boys. "You can't put Hiccup in charge, sir, he's **USELESS**."

Hiccup Horrendous Haddock the Third, the

GOBBER the Belch
Idiot in charge of initiation

Hope and Heir to the Tribe of the Hairy Hooligans, wiped his nose miserably on his sleeve. He sank a little deeper into the snow.

"ANYBODY would be better than Hiccup," sneered Snotface Snotlout. "Even Fishlegs would be better than Hiccup."

Fishlegs had a squint that made him as blind as a jellyfish, and an allergy to reptiles.

"SILENCE!" roared Gobber the Belch. "The next boy to speak has limpets for lunch for the next THREE WEEKS!"

There was absolute silence immediately. Limpets are a bit like worms and a bit like snot and a lot less tasty than either.

"Hiccup will be in charge and that is an order!" screamed Gobber, who didn't do noises quieter than screaming. He was a seven-foot giant with a mad glint in his one working eye and a beard like exploding fireworks. Despite the freezing cold he was wearing hairy shorts and a teeny weeny deerskin vest that showed off his lobster-red skin and bulging muscles. He was holding a flaming torch in one gigantic fist.

4

"Hiccup will be leading you, although he is, admittedly, completely useless, because Hiccup is the son of the CHIEF, and that's the way things go with us Vikings. Where do you think you are, the REPUBLIC OF ROME? Anyway, that is the least of your problems today. You are here to prove yourself as a Viking Hero. And it is an ancient tradition of the Hooligan Tribe that you should —" Gobber paused dramatically —

"FIRST CATCH YOUR DRAGON!"

Ohhhhhh suffering scallops, thought Hiccup.

Ohhh suffering scallops

"Our dragons are what set us apart!" bellowed Gobber. "Lesser humans train hawks to hunt for them, horses to carry them. It is only the VIKING HEROES who dare to tame the wildest, most dangerous creatures on Earth."

Gobber spat solemnly into the snow. "There are three parts to the Dragon Initiation Test. The first and most dangerous part is a test of your courage and skill at burglary. If you wish to enter the Hairy Hooligan Tribe, you must first catch your dragon. And that is WHY," continued Gobber, at full volume, "I have brought you to this scenic spot. Take a look at Wild Dragon Cliff itself."

The ten boys tipped their heads backward.

The cliff loomed dizzyingly high above them, black and sinister. In summer you could barely even see the cliff as dragons of all shapes and sizes swarmed over it, snapping and biting and sending up a cacophony of noise that could be heard all over Berk.

But in winter the dragons were hibernating and the cliff fell silent, except for the ominous, low rumble of their snores. Hiccup could feel the vibrations through his sandals.

"Now," said Gobber, "do you notice those four caves about halfway up the cliff, grouped roughly in the shape of a skull?"

The boys nodded.

"Inside the cave that would be the right eye of the skull is the Dragon Nursery, where there are, AT THIS VERY MOMENT, three thousand young dragons having their last few weeks of winter sleep."

"OOOOOOOH," muttered the boys excitedly.

6

Hiccup swallowed hard. He happened to know considerably more about dragons than anybody else there. Ever since he was a small boy, he'd been fascinated by the creatures. He'd spent hour after long hour dragon watching in secret. (Dragon-spotters were thought to be geeks and nerds, hence the need for secrecy.) And what Hiccup had learned about dragons told him that walking into a cave with three thousand dragons in it was an act of madness.

No one else seemed too concerned, however.

"In a few minutes I want you to take one of these baskets and start climbing the cliff," commanded Gobber the Belch. "Once you are at the cave entrance, you are on your own. I am too large to squeeze my way into the tunnels that lead to the Dragon Nursery. You will enter the cave QUIETLY— and that means you too, Wartihog, unless you want to become the first spring meal for three thousand hungry dragons, HA HA HA HA!"

Gobber laughed heartily at his little joke, then continued. "Dragons this size are normally fairly harmless to man, but in these numbers they will set upon you like piranhas. There'd be nothing left of even a fatso like you, Wartihog — just a pile of bones

DRAGON BASKET

DRAGON goes in HERE

and your helmet. HA HA HA HA! So . . . you will walk QUIETLY through the cave and each boy will steal ONE sleeping dragon. Lift the dragon GENTLY from the rock and place it in your basket. Any questions so far?"

Nobody had any questions.

"In the unlikely event that you DO wake the dragons — and you would have to be IDIOTICALLY STUPID to do so — run like thunder for the entrance to the cave. Dragons do not like cold weather and the snow will probably stop them in their tracks."

Probably? thought Hiccup. *Oh, well,* that's *reassuring.*

"I suggest that you spend a little time choosing your dragon. It is important to get one the correct size. This will be the dragon that hunts fish for you, and pulls down deer for you. You will catch the dragon that will carry you into battle later on, when you are much older and a Warrior of the Tribe. But, nonetheless, you want an impressive animal, so a rough guide would be, choose the biggest creature that will fit into your basket. Don't linger for TOO long in there —"

Linger??? thought Hiccup. *In a cave full of three thousand sleeping* DRAGONS?

"I need not tell you," Gobber continued cheerfully, "that if you return to this spot *without* a dragon, it is hardly worth coming back at all. Anybody who FAILS this task will be put into immediate exile. The Hairy Hooligan Tribe has no use for FAILURES. Only the strong can belong."

Unhappily, Hiccup looked round at the distant horizon. Nothing but snow and sea as far as the eye could see. Exile didn't look too promising, either.

"RIGHT," said Gobber briskly. "Each boy take a basket to put their dragon in and we'll get going."

9

The boys rushed to get their baskets, chattering happily and excitedly.

"I'm going to get one of those Monstrous Nightmare ones with the extra-extendable claws. They're really scary," boasted Snotlout.

"Oh shut up, Snotlout, you can't," said Speedifist. "Only Hiccup can have a Monstrous Nightmare, you have to be the son of a chief." Hiccup's father was Stoick the Vast, the fearsome chief of the Hairy Hooligan tribe.

"HICCUP?" sneered Snotlout. "If he's as useless at this as he is at Bashyball, we'll be lucky if he even gets one of the Basic Browns."

The Basic Brown was the most common type of dragon, a serviceable beast but without much glamour.

"SHUDDUP AND GET INTO LINE YOU MISERABLE TADPOLES!" yelled Gobber the Belch.

The boys scrambled into their places, baskets on their backs, and stood to attention. Gobber walked along the line, lighting the torch that each boy held in front of him from the great flare in his hand.

"IN HALF AN HOUR'S TIME YOU WILL BE A VIKING WARRIOR, WITH YOUR FAITHFUL SERPENT AT YOUR SIDE . . .

THE COMMON OR GARDEN and THE BASIC BROWN

The Common or Garden and the Basic Brown are so similar that they can be dealt with together. These are the most familiar breeds – the ones we instantly think of when we say "dragons." They are poor hunters, but they are easy to train. These dragons are the best kind for family pets, although, as with a lion or a tiger, they should never be left unsupervised with very young children.

The Common or Garden
or
Basic Brown

~ STATISTICS ~

COLORS: Green and yellow, all shades of brown

ARMED WITH: Basic teeth and claws **3**

DEFENSES: Prickly spines **2**

RADAR: None **0**

POISON: None **0**

HUNTING ABILITY: Lethargic hunters **3**

SPEED: Swift in retreat **8**

FEAR AND FIGHT FACTOR:
Good when angry **4**

... OR BREAKFASTING WITH WODEN IN VALHALLA WITH DRAGONS' TEETH IN YOUR BOTTOM!" screamed Gobber with horrible enthusiasm.

"DEATH OR GLORY!" yelled Gobber.

"DEATH OR GLORY!" yelled eight boys back at him fanatically.

Death, thought Hiccup and Fishlegs, sadly.

Gobber paused dramatically, with the horn to his lips.

I think this could possibly be the worst moment of my life SO FAR, thought Hiccup to himself as he waited for the blast of the horn. *And if they shout much louder, we're going to wake up those dragons before we even START.*

"PARRRRRRRRRP!" Gobber blew the horn.

13

2. INSIDE THE DRAGON NURSERY

You have probably guessed by now that Hiccup was not your natural Viking Hero.

For a start, he didn't LOOK like a Hero. Somebody like Snotlout, for instance, was tall, muscley, covered in skeleton tattoos, and already had the beginnings of a small moustache. This consisted of a few straggly yellow hairs clinging to his upper lip and was deeply unpleasant to look at, but still impressively manly for a boy not yet thirteen.

Hiccup was on the small side and had the kind of face that was almost entirely unmemorable. He DID have Heroic Hair, which was a very bright red and

snotlout

14

Dogsbreath the Duhbrain

stood up vertically however much you
tried to wet it down with seawater.
But nobody ever saw that because it
was hidden under his helmet
most of the time.

You would NEVER have
picked Hiccup out of those ten
boys to be the Hero of this story.
Snotlout was good at everything
and a natural leader. Dogsbreath
was as tall as his father and could
do amusing things like farting
to the tune of the Berk national
anthem.

Hiccup was just absolutely
average, the kind of unremarkable, skinny, freckled boy who was easy
to overlook in a crowd.

So, when Gobber blew the horn and moved out
of sight to find a comfortable rock to sit on and eat his
mussel-and-tomato sandwich, Snotlout pushed Hiccup
out of the way and took charge.

"Okay, listen up, boys," he whispered in a
menacing fashion. "I'M in charge, not the Useless. And

anybody who objects gets a knuckle sandwich from Dogsbreath the Duhbrain."

"Ugh," grunted Dogsbreath, pounding his fists together in happy excitement. Dogsbreath was Snotlout's chief sidekick and a great, big gorilla of a boy.

"Bash him, Dogsbreath, to show what I mean . . ."

Dogsbreath was delighted to oblige. He gave Hiccup a shove that sent him sprawling headfirst into the snow, then ground his face in it.

"Pay attention!" hissed Snotlout. The boys dragged their eyes away from Dogsbreath and Hiccup and paid attention. "Rope yourselves together. The best climber should go first . . ."

"Well, that's YOU of course, Snotlout," said Fishlegs. "You're the best at everything, aren't you?"

Snotlout looked at Fishlegs suspiciously. It was difficult to tell whether Fishlegs was laughing at him or not, because of his squint.

"That's right, Fishlegs," said Snotlout. "I AM." And, just in case he *had* been laughing at him: "Bash him, Dogsbreath!"

While Dogsbreath pushed Fishlegs down to join Hiccup in the snow, everybody started roping themselves together.

Hiccup and Fishlegs were the last to be tied on, just behind a flushed and triumphant Dogsbreath.

"Oh, brilliant," muttered Fishlegs. "I'm about to enter a cave full of man-eating reptiles tied up to eight complete maniacs."

"If we *get* to the cave . . ." said Hiccup nervously, looking up at the sheer black cliff.

Hiccup put the lighted torch between his teeth to leave his hands free, and started climbing after the others.

♥ ♥ ♥

It was a perilous climb. The rocks were slippery with snow and the other boys were thoroughly overexcited, making the ascent far too quickly. At one point Clueless missed his footing and fell — luckily onto Dogsbreath, who caught him by the back of the trousers and heaved him back on to the rock again, before he brought the whole lot of them down.

When they finally made it to the mouth of the cave, Hiccup looked down briefly at the sea pounding the rocks way below, and swallowed very hard . . .

"Untie the ropes!" ordered Snotlout, his eyes popping with excitement at the thought of the dangers to come. "Hiccup goes into the cave first because

HE is the son of the Chief. . . ." He sneered. "And, if any of the dragons ARE awake, he'll be the first to know about it! Once we're in the cave, it's every man for himself. Only the strong can belong. . . ."

Although he wasn't your usual mindless thug of a Hooligan, Hiccup wasn't a wimp, either. Being frightened is not the same as being a coward. Maybe he *was* as brave as anyone else there, because he went to catch a dragon *despite* knowing what dragons are like. And, when he had climbed perilously to the mouth of the cave and had found that inside there was a long, twisty tunnel, he *still* went down it, despite not being too keen on long, twisty tunnels with dragons at the end of them.

The tunnel was dripping and clammy. At times it was high enough for the boys to walk upright. Then it would close down into narrow, claustrophobic holes that the boys could only just squeeze through, squirming on their stomachs, with the flares held in their mouths.

After ten long minutes of walking and crawling into the heart of the cliff, the stench of dragon — a salty stink of seaweed and old mackerel heads — got stronger and stronger, until finally it became unbearable and the tunnel opened out into an enormous cavern.

The cavern was full of more dragons than Hiccup could ever have imagined existed.

They were every possible color and size, and they included all the species that Hiccup had heard of, and quite a few more that he hadn't.

Hiccup started sweating as he looked around him at pile after pile of the animals, draped over every available surface; even hanging upside down from the roof like giant bats. They were all fast asleep, and most of them were snoring in unison. This was a sound so loud and so deep that it seemed to penetrate right into Hiccup's body and vibrate around his soft insides, churning his stomach and bowels, and forcing his heart to beat at the same slow dragon pulse.

If one, just *one*, of these countless creatures were to wake up, it would raise the alarm to the others and the boys would meet a horrible death. Hiccup had once seen a deer that had wandered too close to Wild Dragon Cliff torn to pieces in a matter of minutes . . .

Hiccup closed his eyes. "I will NOT think about it," he said to himself. "I WILL NOT."

None of the other boys were thinking about it. Ignorance is very useful in such circumstances. Their eyes were popping with excitement as they walked through the cave, hands over their noses to keep out the revolting smell, looking for the biggest dragon they could find that would fit in their basket.

They left the torches in a pile at the entrance. The cavern was already well-lit by the Glowworms — huge, sluggish animals dotted here and there that shone with a steady yet dim fluorescence, like a low-watt lightbulb. And the Flamehuffers gave off extra little bursts of light that flickered on and off as they breathed in and out.

Predictably, most of the boys headed toward the plug-uglies of the dragon world.

Snotlout made a big fuss about grabbing a vicious-looking Monstrous Nightmare, smiling nastily at Hiccup as he did so. Snotlout was the son of Baggy-bum the Beerbelly, Stoick the Vast's younger brother. He was intending to get rid of Hiccup sometime in the future so that he, Snotlout, would become Chief of the Hairy Hooligan Tribe. And a gruesome and terrifying Chief, as Snotlout meant to be, would need a properly awesome dragon.

Wartihog and Dogsbreath got into a loudly whispered fight over a Gronckle, a heavily-armored brute with fangs like kitchen knives sticking out in such numbers that it couldn't keep its mouth shut. Dogsbreath won, then managed to drop it as he was trying to bundle it into his basket. The weaponry of the beast made a horribly loud clatter as it landed on the floor of the cavern.

The Gronckle opened its evil, crocodile eyes.

Everybody held their breath.

The Gronckle stared ahead. It was difficult to tell from its blank expression whether it was awake or fast asleep. Hiccup realized, in an agony of suspense, that the gossamer-thin third eyelid was still down.

And there it stayed for a few heart-stopping moments, until . . .

It slowly closed its upper eyelids again.

Amazingly, not one of the other dragons woke up. A few grumbled groggily before making themselves comfy again. But most were in such a stupor that they barely even stirred.

Hiccup let out his breath. Maybe these dragons were so dead to the world that *nothing* would wake them from their slumber.

THE GRONCKLE

The Gronckle is the plug-ugly of the dragon world. But what it lacks in looks, it makes up for on the battlefield. They can be slow and, dare I say it, stupid ~ and sometimes they get so fat that they are unable to take off. They are also prone to dragon acne.

Extra thick Skull

a nasty case of dragon Acne

~ STATISTICS ~

COLORS: Snot green, bogey beige, pooey brown.
ARMED WITH: All the best in dragon weaponry. Fangs like daggers, extra spike on neck, ball with spikes on end of tail **8**
DEFENSES: Super-thick, flame-proof and scratch-proof skin **9**
RADAR: None **0**
POISON: None **0**
HUNTING ABILITY: Gronckles are slow to maneuver in the air **0**
SPEED: See above **5**
FEAR AND FIGHT FACTOR: Terrifying in action **9**

He swallowed hard, muttered a prayer to Loki, the patron saint of sneaky exploits, and edged forward cautiously to grab the most unconscious-looking dragon, so he could get out of this nightmare as fast as possible.

♦ ♦ ♦

It is a little-known fact that dragons grow colder the deeper they sleep.

It is even possible for dragons to go into a sleep coma in which they are icy cold, with no obvious pulse, or breath, or heartbeat. They can stay in this state for centuries, and only a highly skilled expert can tell from looking at them if they are alive or dead.

But a dragon who is awake or lightly sleeping is very warm indeed, like bread that has just come out of the oven.

Hiccup found one that was about the right size and fairly cool to the touch and maneuvered it into his basket as quickly and carefully as he could. It was a very basic Basic Brown, but at that moment Hiccup could not have cared less. Even though it was barely half-grown, it was surprisingly heavy.

"I DID it, I DID it, I DID it!" he chanted happily

to himself. At least he wasn't going to be the only boy in the class who didn't have a dragon. Everybody seemed to have gotten themselves one by now and they were all making their way quietly toward the exit. Everybody, that was, except for . . .

Fishlegs, who was already covered in a bright red, itchy rash, and was at that very moment approaching a pile of knottily entangled Nadders on very loud tiptoes.

Fishlegs was even worse at burglary than Dogs-breath.

Hiccup stopped dead in his tracks. "Don't do it, Fishlegs — PLEASE don't do it!" he whispered.

But Fishlegs was fed up with Snotlout's taunting and of being sneered at and jeered at. He was going to get himself a really cool dragon that all the other boys would respect.

Squinting so hard he could barely see the pile of dragons, his eyes streaming, and scratching himself violently, Fishlegs reached slowly toward the bottom-most dragon, took one leg in his hand, and gently . . . yanked.

The entire pile came crashing down in a furious

tangle of limbs and wings and ears. Every boy in the cavern gave a horrified gasp.

Most of the Nadders snapped crossly at each other before settling back down to sleep.

One brute bigger than the others opened his eyes and blinked a few times.

Hiccup noted, with great relief, that the third eyelid was still down.

The boys waited for the eyes to close.

And then Fishlegs sneezed.

Four GIGANTIC sneezes that went echoing and bouncing off the cavern walls.

The big Nadder stared sightlessly ahead, frozen like a dragon statue.

But ve-ry faintly, an ominous purring noise began in his throat.

And ve-ry slowly . . .

. . . the third eyelid slid upward.

"Uh-oh," whispered Hiccup.

The Nadder's head suddenly whipped round to face Fishlegs, its yellow cat's eyes snapping into focus on the boy. It unfolded its wings to their greatest extent and stealthily advanced, like a panther about to

spring. It opened its mouth wide enough to show the forked dragon tongue and . . .

"R-R-R-U-U-U-U-U-N-N-N!" shouted Hiccup, grabbing Fishlegs's arm and dragging him away.

The boys ran for the exit tunnel. Fishlegs and Hiccup were the last to get there.

There was no time to pick up the torches, so they were running in the pitch dark. The basket with the Basic Brown dragon in it was bumping on Hiccup's back.

They had two minutes' start on the dragons because it took a while for the first dragon to wake everybody else up. But Hiccup could hear a furious roaring and flapping as the dragons started to pour into the tunnel after the boys.

He ran a little faster.

The dragons could move faster than the boys because they could see better in the dark, but they were held up when the tunnel got smaller, and they had to fold their wings up to squirm through.

"I . . . haven't . . . got . . . a . . . dragon," panted Fishlegs, a couple of paces behind Hiccup.

"That," said Hiccup, as he scrambled frantically on his elbows through a narrow bit, "is the LEAST . . . *ow* . . . of our problems. They're gaining on us!"

"No . . . dragon," repeated Fishlegs stubbornly.

"Oh, for THOR'S SAKE," snapped Hiccup.

He thrust his basket into Fishlegs's arms and grabbed the empty one from Fishlegs's back. "Have MINE, then. Wait here."

And Hiccup turned and went back through the narrow bit even though the roaring was getting louder and closer by the second.

"WHAT . . . ARE . . . YOU . . . DOING???" screamed Fishlegs, frantically dancing up and down on the spot.

Hiccup came back through the hole again precious moments later. Fishlegs grabbed hold of an arm to help haul him through.

The Flight from the Dragon Nursery

They could hear a horrible snuffling that sounded as if the nose of a dragon had entered the other end of the hole. Hiccup bunged a rock at it and it squealed indignantly.

They turned a corner and suddenly they could see light from outside at the end of the final tunnel.

Fishlegs went first, but, just as Hiccup was kneeling down to follow, a dragon pounced on him with a flap and a shriek. Hiccup hit it and it fell back enough for him to crawl toward the light. Another dragon — or maybe the same one — sank its fangs into Hiccup's calf. He was so desperate to get out he dragged the animal through with him.

As soon as Hiccup's head and shoulders were through into the light, there was Gobber. He grabbed Hiccup under the armpits and hauled him out, dragons pouring after him.

"JUMP!" yelled Gobber, as he stunned a dragon with one blow of his mighty fist.

"What do you *mean,* JUMP??" Hiccup hesitated as he looked down at the dizzying drop into the sea.

"No time to climb down," panted Gobber, banging a couple of dragons' heads together, and bouncing three more off his gigantic belly. "JUMP!!!"

Hiccup closed his eyes and leaped off the cliff.

As he plunged through the air, the dragon that was attached to his leg released its jaws with a squawk of alarm and flew off.

Hiccup was traveling at such speed by the time he hit the water that it didn't feel like water at all, more like something hard and painful, and so cold that he nearly passed out.

He spluttered to the surface, amazed to find that he didn't appear to be dead, and was immediately drenched by the gigantic splash of Gobber the Belch landing a couple of feet away from him.

Shrieking furiously, the dragons swarmed out of the cave and dive-bombed the floating Vikings.

Hiccup pulled his helmet as far down as it would go. There were horrible scraping sounds as dragons' talons raked across the metal. Another one landed, hissing, on the water right in front of Hiccup's face. It took off again with a screech when it felt how cold the sea was. The dragons didn't like flying through the snow and, with relief, Hiccup watched as they flew back to scream terrible dragon insults in Dragonese from the warmth of the cave entrance.

Gobber started to pull the boys out of the sea

and onto the rocks. Viking boys are strong swimmers, but it is difficult to keep afloat when you have a basket full of trapped, terrified dragons on your back. Hiccup was the last to be saved — just in time, as the cold was beginning to put him to sleep.

Well, at least that wasn't DEATH, thought Hiccup as Gobber grabbed him by the neck to rescue him, nearly drowning him again in the process — *but it certainly wasn't GLORY, either.*

3. HEROES OR EXILES

The boys scrambled over the slimy pebbles at the edge of the beach and back up Madman's Gully, the gorge they had climbed through a couple of hours before. This was a narrow crack in the cliffs filled with large rocks. They tried to move as quickly as they could, but this is difficult when you are slipping and sliding over huge stones covered in ice, and they made painfully slow progress.

A dragon that *hadn't* been put off by the snow came shrieking down into the gorge. He landed on Wartihog's back and started savaging him, sinking his fangs into Wartihog's shoulder and ripping red lines into his arms. Gobber bashed the dragon on the nose with the handle of his axe, and the dragon let go and flapped away.

But a whole wave of dragons replaced him, pouring into the canyon with awful, rasping cries, fire shooting from their nostrils and melting the snow before them, talons spread wickedly as they swooped downward.

Gobber stood, legs wide apart, and whirled his big, double-headed axe. He threw back his great,

hairy head and yelled a terrible primeval yell, that
echoed down the sides of the gorge and made the
hairs on the back of Hiccup's neck stick straight up
like the spines on a sea urchin.

Individually, dragons tend to have a healthy sense
of self-preservation, but they are braver when they
hunt in packs. They knew now that they had the ad-
vantage of massive numbers, so they didn't check their
flying for an instant. They just kept on coming.

Gobber let go of the axe.

Spinning end to end, the axe soared up through
the softly falling snow. It hit the biggest dragon of
the lot, killing him instantly, and then kept on going,
landing in a snow-drift hundreds of feet away and
disappearing.

This made the rest of the dragons think a bit.
Some of them scrambled over each other in their
haste to fly away, yelping like dogs. The others came to

a halt, hovering uncertainly, screaming defiance but keeping their distance.

"Waste of a good axe," grunted Gobber. "Keep going, boys, they could come back!"

Hiccup needed no encouragement to keep going. As soon as he got out of the gorge and onto the marshy land behind it, he broke into a stumbling run, every now and then falling flat on his face in the snow.

Some time later, when Gobber reckoned they were a safe distance from Wild Dragon Cliff, he yelled at the boys to stop.

Very carefully he counted heads again, to check he hadn't lost anybody. Gobber had spent an unpleasant ten minutes standing at the mouth of the dragons' cave wondering why there was such a terrible racket and what he was going to say to Stoick the Vast if he lost his precious son and heir for good.

Something Tactful and Sensitive, he supposed, but Tact and Sensitivity were not Gobber's strong points, and he took the first five minutes to come up with "Hiccup copped it. SORRY," and then spent the second five minutes tearing his beard out.

Consequently, although secretly mightily relieved, he was not in a Good Mood and, as soon as he could get his breath back, he exploded all over the place, as the boys stood, shivering violently, in a bedraggled line.

"NEVER . . . in FOURTEEN YEARS . . . have I come across such a load of HOPELESS BARNACLES as you lot. WHICH OF YOU USELESS MOLLUSKS WAS RESPONSIBLE FOR WAKING UP THE DRAGONS????"

"I was," said Hiccup. Which wasn't strictly true.

"Oh, that's BRILLIANT," bellowed Gobber, "just BRILLIANT. Our Future Leader shows off his magnificent Leadership Skills. At the tender age of ten and a half he does his best to annihilate himself and the rest of you in A SIMPLE MILITARY EXERCISE!"

Snotlout sniggered.

"You find something amusing about that, Snotlout?" asked Gobber, with dangerous softness. "EVERYBODY IS ON LIMPET RATIONS FOR THE NEXT THREE WEEKS."

The boys groaned.

"Smart work, Hiccup," sneered Snotlout. "I can't wait to see you in action on the battlefield."

"SILENCE!" yelled Gobber. "THIS IS YOUR

INITIATION, NOT A DAY OUT IN THE COUNTRY! SILENCE, OR YOU'LL BE LUNCHING ON LUGWORMS FOR THE REST OF YOUR LIVES!"

"Now," continued Gobber, more calmly, "although that was an absolute mess, it wasn't a total disaster. I PRESUME that you do all HAVE a dragon after that fiasco . . . ?"

"Yes," chorused the boys.

Fishlegs took a sideways glance at Hiccup, who was staring straight ahead.

"Lucky for you," said Gobber, ominously. "So you have all passed the first part of the Dragon Test. There are, however, still two parts that you have to complete before you can become full members of the Tribe. Your next task will be to train this dragon yourself. This will be a test of the force of your personality. You will assert your will over this wild creature and show it who is Master. Your dragon will be expected to obey simple commands such as "go" and "stay," and hunt fish for you in the way that dragons have hunted for the Sons of Thor since anybody can remember. If you are worried about the training process, you should study a book called *How to Train Your Dragon* by

Professor Yobbish, which you will find in the fireplace of the Great Hall."

Suddenly Gobber looked very pleased with himself. "I stole that book from the Meathead Public Library myself," he said modestly, regarding his very black fingernails. "From right under the nose of the Hairy Scary Librarian . . . He never noticed a thing . . . Now THAT'S burglary for you. . . ."

Wartihog put up his hand. "What happens if we can't read, sir?"

"No boasting, Wartihog!" boomed Gobber. "Get some idiot to read it for you. Your dragons will begin to go back to sleep, because this is still their hibernation time" — some of the dragons had, indeed, gone very quiet inside the baskets — "so take them home and put them in a warm place. They should wake up in the next couple of weeks. You will then have only FOUR MONTHS to prepare for Initiation Day at the Thor's-day Thursday Celebrations, and the final part of your Test. If, on that day, you can prove that you have trained your dragon to the satisfaction of myself and other elders of the Tribe, you can finally call yourself a Hooligan of Berk."

The boys stood very tall and tried to look like proper Hooligans.

"HEROES OR EXILE!" yelled Gobber the Belch.

"HEROES OR EXILE!" yelled eight boys fanatically back at him.

Exile, thought Hiccup and Fishlegs sadly.

♥ ♥ ♥

"I . . . hate . . . being . . . a . . . Viking," panted Fishlegs to Hiccup as they stumbled back through the bracken to the Hooligan village.

You didn't really *walk* on the island of Berk, you *waded* — through heather or bracken or mud or snow, which clung on to your legs and made them difficult to lift. It was the sort of country where the sea and the land were always falling into one another and getting mixed up. The island was shot through with holes burrowed by the water, a maze of criss-crossing underground streams. You could put your foot on a solid-looking piece of grass and find yourself disappearing up to your thigh in black, sticky mud. You could be making your way through the ferns and suddenly find yourself fording a river, waist-high and icy cold.

The boys were already soaked to the skin with

seawater, and now the snow had turned to horizontal driving rain, blowing in their faces with the strength of one of the gale-force winds that were always shrieking across the salty wastelands of Berk.

"A narrow escape from horrible death first thing on Thursday morning," complained Fishlegs, "followed by complete rejection by the junior half of the Tribe . . . Nobody's going to talk to me for YEARS after this — except for you, of course, Hiccup, but then you're just a weirdo like me — "

"Thank you," said Hiccup.

"And on top of everything," continued Fishlegs bitterly, "a two-mile run carrying a deranged dragon on my back" — the basket on Fishlegs' back was plunging wildly from side to side as the dragon inside tried man-

ically to get out — "and only a dinner of horrible limpets to look forward to at the end of it."

Hiccup agreed that it wasn't a delicious prospect.

"You can have this dragon back if you like, Hiccup. I warn you, they're filthy heavy when they're wet and angry," said Fishlegs, miserably. "Gobber is going to go off like a typhoon when he finds out you haven't got a dragon."

"But I HAVE got one," said Hiccup.

Fishlegs stopped and began to take the basket off his back. "I know it IS yours REALLY," he sighed wearily. "I think I'll just go straight past the village and keep on running till I reach somewhere civilized. Rome perhaps. I've always wanted to go to Rome. And I haven't got a hope in Valhalla of passing Initiation anyway, so —"

"No, I've got *another* one, in my basket," Hiccup insisted.

Fishlegs' jaw dropped open in disbelief.

"I got it when I went back into the tunnel," explained Hiccup.

"Well, blister my barnacles," said Fishlegs. "How in Thor's name did you know it was there? It was so dark you couldn't see the horns in front of you."

"It was weird," said Hiccup. "I sort of sensed it when we were running down the tunnel. I couldn't see anything, but as we were passing, I just *knew* there was a dragon there, and that it was meant to be MY dragon. I was going to ignore it, actually, because we were in a bit of a hurry, but then you said about not having a dragon and I went back, and . . . there it was, lying on this shelf in the tunnel, just as I'd imagined it would be."

"Well, jigger my jellyfish," said Fishlegs, and the boys started running again.

Hiccup was bruised all over, shaking from shock, and he had a nasty dragon wound in his calf, which was stinging like crazy from the saltwater. He was freezing cold and there was an irritating bit of seaweed in one of his sandals.

He was also a bit worried because he knew he should not have risked his life trying to get a dragon for Fishlegs. This was not the act of a Viking Hero. A Viking Hero would know not to intervene between Fishlegs and his Fate.

On the other hand, Hiccup had been worrying about Dragon-catching Day for longer than he could remember. He had been sure he would be the only one

to come back without a dragon, and shame, embarrassment, and awful exile would follow.

And now, here he was: a Viking warrior WITH a
dragon.

So, on the whole, he was feeling fairly pleased
with himself.

Things were looking up.

♦ ♦ ♦

"You know, Hiccup," said Fishlegs a little later, as the
wooden fortifications of the village appeared on the
horizon, "that sounds like Fate, you sensing the dragon
was there like that. This could be Meant to Be. You
could have some sort of wonder-dragon in there.
Something that makes a Monstrous Nightmare look
like a flying frog! You are the son and heir of Chief
Stoick after all, and it's about time Fate came in
with a sign about your destiny."

The boys stopped, puffing with exhaustion.

"Oh, I'm sure it's just a Common or Garden that
wandered away from the rest," said Hiccup, trying to
sound careless but unable to keep the excitement out
of his voice. *He could have something marvelous in there!*

Maybe Old Wrinkly was right. Old Wrinkly was
Hiccup's grandfather on his mother's side. He had

taken up soothsaying in his old age and he kept on telling Hiccup how he had looked into the future and that Hiccup was destined for great things.

This amazing dragon could be the beginning of his transformation from ordinary old Hiccup, who wasn't particularly good at anything, into a Hero of the Future!

Hiccup took the basket off his back and paused before opening it.

"It's very still, isn't it?" said Fishlegs, suddenly less certain of the Fate theory. "I mean, it isn't moving at all in there. Are you sure it's alive?"

"It's just very deeply asleep," said Hiccup. "It was stone cold when I picked it up."

Suddenly he had a strong feeling that the gods were on his side. He KNEW that this dragon was alive.

With trembling fingers, Hiccup undid the latch, took off the lid of the basket, and peered in. Fishlegs joined him.

Things weren't looking so good anymore.

There, curled up fast asleep in the bottom of the basket in a tangled dragon knot, lay perhaps the most common Common or Garden Dragon Hiccup had ever seen.

how SMALL it was. The most extraordinary thing about this dragon was

Absolutely the *only* extraordinary thing about this dragon was how extraordinarily SMALL it was.

In this it was *truly* extraordinary.

Most dragons that the Vikings used for hunting purposes were about the size of a Labrador retriever. The adolescent dragons the boys were collecting weren't quite that big, but they *were* nearly fully grown. This dragon was more comparable to a West Highland Terrier.

Hiccup couldn't think how he had overlooked this when he picked the dragon up in the tunnel. He supposed, miserably, that it was rather a pressured moment, what with three thousand dragons trying to kill him at the time. And dragons in a deep Sleep Coma do tend to weigh more than they do when they're awake.

"Well," said Hiccup at last, "that's a sign, if you like. You reach for a Deadly Nadder and what do you get? A Basic Brown. I grab a dragon in the dark and what do I get? A Common or Garden. The thing is, the gods are telling us we're Common or Garden folk, Fishlegs. You and I, we're not *meant* to be Heroes."

"It doesn't matter about ME . . . ," said Fishlegs,

"but you *are* meant to be a Hero. Remember? Son of the Chief and all that? And you *will* be one, I know you will. . . ."

Fishlegs put the basket back on Hiccup's back and they trudged toward the village gates together.

". . . At least, I sincerely HOPE you will. I don't want to be following Snotlout into battle. You've got more ideas about military tactics in your little finger than Snotlout has in his whole fat head. . . ."

While that may have been true, not only was Hiccup *not* about to be the future star of Dragon training — but with this particular dragon it was even going to be difficult for him to take his familiar place fading into the background.

It was so small it was going to make him look ridiculous.

It was so small that Snotlout was going to have some very unpleasant things to say about it.

4. HOW TO TRAIN YOUR DRAGON

"HA HA HA HA!"

Snotlout was laughing so hard that he hadn't managed to say anything at all.

The boys were hanging about the village gates, taking the opportunity to show off the dragons that they had caught. Hiccup had tried to walk through without being noticed, but Snotlout had stopped him.

"Let's see what pathetic creature Hiccup has got," said Snotlout, and took off the lid.

"Oh, this is BRILLIANT — look at it!" said Snotlout, when he finally got his breath back from laughing. "What IS it, Hiccup? A brown bunny rabbit with wings? A flower fairy? A fluffy flying frog? Gather round everybody and see the magnificent animal that Our Future Leader has caught himself!"

"Oh, Hiccup, you are *useless,*" crowed Speedifist. "You're the son of a CHIEF, for Thor's sake. Why didn't you get one of those new Monstrous Nightmares with the six-foot wing-span and the extra-extendable claws? They're really mean killers, they are."

"*I* have one," grinned Snotlout, gesturing to the terrifying-looking, flame-red animal fast asleep in his basket. "I think I shall call her FIREWORM. What are you going to call yours, Hiccup? Sweetums? Sugarlips? Babyface?"

Hiccup's dragon took this particular moment to give a huge yawn, opening his tiny mouth wide to reveal a flickering, forked tongue, very pink gums, and ABSOLUTELY NO TEETH AT ALL.

Snotlout laughed so hard, Speedifist had to hold him upright.

"TOOTHLESS!" cried Snotlout. "Hiccup has found himself the only TOOTHLESS dragon in the uncivilized world! This is too good. Hiccup the USELESS and his dragon, TOOTHLESS!"

Fishlegs leaped to Hiccup's defense.

"Well, *you* are not allowed that Monstrous Nightmare that you've got there, Snotface Snotlout. Only the son of a Chief is allowed a Monstrous Nightmare. That Fireworm dragon is Hiccup's, by right."

Snotlout's eyes narrowed. He grabbed Fishlegs's arm and twisted it viciously behind his back.

"Nobody's listening to you, you plankton-hearted, fish-legged, disaster area," sneered Snotlout. "Thanks to you and your sniveling, sneezing disability, that whole military operation was nearly a total disaster. When I'm Chief of this Tribe the first thing I'm going to do is boot anybody with a pathetic allergy like yours straight out into exile. You're not fit to be a Hooligan!"

Fishlegs went very white in the face, but he still managed to gasp out, "But you are NOT going to be Chief of this Tribe. HICCUP is going to be Chief of this Tribe."

Snotlout dropped Fishlegs's arm and advanced menacingly on Hiccup.

"Oh, he is, is he?" jeered Snotlout. "So, I'm not allowed that Monstrous Nightmare, am I? Our Future Leader is keeping very quiet about it, isn't he? Come on, Hiccup, I'm stealing your inheritance. What are you going to do about it, then, eh?"

The boys all looked solemn. Snotlout really had broken an ancient Viking rule.

"Hiccup should challenge you for the dragon," said Fishlegs slowly, and everybody swiveled around to look expectantly at Hiccup.

"Oh, brilliant," muttered Hiccup under his breath. "Thank you, Fishlegs. My day just gets better and better."

Snotlout was a great brute of a boy who didn't really need Dogsbreath's help when it came to bashing people up. He wore specially constructed, bronze-tipped sandals in order to cause maximum damage when kicking people. Hiccup tried to stay out of his way as much as he possibly could.

But he couldn't ignore this insult to his status, now that Fishlegs had helpfully pointed it out, without looking like a coward in front of the other boys. And if you became known as a coward in the Hooligan Tribe, you might as well go the whole hog and wear a pale pink jerkin, take up playing the harp, and change your name to Ermintrude.

"I challenge you, Snotface Snotlout, for the dragon, Fireworm, who is mine by right," said Hiccup, trying to hide his reluctance by speaking as loudly and formally as he could.

"I accept your challenge," said Snotlout super-fast, grinning all over his horrid, smug face. "Axes or fists?"

"Fists," said Hiccup. Because axes were a REALLY bad idea.

"I shall look forward to showing you how a real Future Hero fights," said Snotlout, and then he remembered something, "AFTER the Initiation thing on Thor'sday Thursday, though. I don't want to stub my toe or anything while I'm kicking you all around the village."

"Hiccup might win," Fishlegs pointed out.

"OF COURSE he won't win," boasted Snotlout. "Look at my sporting ability, my Viking courage, my capacity for mindless violence. I shall win just as surely as I shall be Chief of this Tribe one day. I mean, look at my dragon and then look at HIS dragon." He pointed mockingly at Toothless. "The gods have spoken. It's only a matter of time.

"In the meantime," Snotlout carried on, "I shall live in fear of being gummed to death by Hiccup's terrifying, toothless terrapin."

And Snotlout sauntered off in a lordly fashion, giving Hiccup a nasty kick on the shins as he did so.

♥ ♥ ♥

"Sorry about the challenge," Fishlegs apologized, after they had left the baskets with the dragons in them under their beds at their homes.

"Oh, don't worry about it," said Hiccup. "Somebody would have gotten me to do it anyway. You know how they all love a fight."

Fishlegs and Hiccup were going to the Great Hall to look for the book Gobber had recommended: *How to Train Your Dragon*, by Professor Yobbish.

"As it happens," confided Hiccup, "I know a bit about dragons already, but I haven't the foggiest clue how to start training one. I would have said they were virtually untrainable. I'm really looking forward to getting some tips."

The Great Hall was a hullabaloo of young barbarians fighting, yelling, and playing the popular Viking game of Bashyball, which was a very violent contact sport with lots of contact and very few rules.

Hiccup and Fishlegs found the book tucked away in the fireplace, practically in the fire.

Hiccup had never noticed it before.

He opened the book.

(I have included a basic replica of *How to Train Your Dragon,* by Professor Yobbish, here — in order that you can share the experience with Hiccup of opening that book for the first time, full of hope and interest and expectation. You will have to imagine that the cover is unusually thick, with huge golden clasps, and that some scribe has covered it in elaborately fancy gilt lettering. It looks very inviting indeed.)

HOW TO TRAIN YOUR DRAGON

—BY—

PROFESSOR YOBBISH
BA, MA Hons, Cantab. Etc.

BIG AXE BOOKS

10th Anniversary Edition

WINNER OF THE
BEST BOOK FOR
BARBARIANS
GOLD AWARD

BEOWULF is a SOFTY

come Heer and say that

MEATHEAD PUBLIC LIBRARY

A note from the Hairy Scary Librarian: Please return this book on or before the last date stamped or I will be VERY ANNOYED. I think you know what I mean.

10 JUNE	789	AD
9 APRIL	835	AD
16 MAY	866	AD

DO NOT REMOVE THIS BOOK OR WE WILL BASH YOU!!!

MY DAD IS TUFFER THAN YOOR

No way → DAD

MY dad coodhav yuur dad for brekfast

ABOUT THE AUTHOR

Professor Yobbish (BA, MA Hons, Cantab. etc.) has spent many years in the wild observing dragons in their natural habitat. This book is the culmination of his research and it is the definitive textbook on the subject of these fascinating creatures.

Professor Yobbish lives alone in a cave on the Isle of Doom. He is the author of *Looking After Your Killer Whale* and *Sharks and Other Great Pets*. He is currently writing a book about butterflies.

CHAPTER THE FIRST (AND LAST)

The Golden Rule of Dragon-Training is to...

YELL AT IT!

(The louder the better.)

THE END.

How would YOU train a dragon?

Look inside for ALL the answers in Professor Yobbish's hugely entertaining and informative book. Follow his simple advice and you will soon be on your way to becoming the Hero you've always wanted to be...

Praise for *How To Train Your Dragon*:

"This book changed my life."
Squidface the Terrible

"A brilliant book." *The Meathead Monthly*

"Nobody yells better than Professor Yobbish. This is a sensitive and well-researched book that contains all the information you need to turn your dragon into a pussy cat." **The** *Hooligan Observer*

"Yobbish is a genius." *The Viking Times*

PRICE: 1 SMALLISH CHICKEN
20 OYSTERS

"THAT'S IT??!" said Hiccup furiously, turning
the book upside down and shaking it, trying to see
whether there was anything other than that single page
of paper inside it.

Hiccup put the book down. His face was
unusually grim.

"Okay, Fishlegs," he said, "unless you're any
better at yelling than I am, we're on our own. We're
going to have to work out our *own* method of dragon
training."

5. A CHAT WITH OLD WRINKLY

The next morning, Hiccup checked the dragon under his bed. It was still asleep.

When his mother, Valhallarama, asked him at breakfast, "How did Initiation go yesterday, dear?" Hiccup said, "Oh, it was fine. I caught my dragon."

"That's nice, dear," Valhallarama replied vaguely.

Stoick the Vast looked up briefly from his bowl and boomed, "EXCELLENT, EXCELLENT," before getting back to the important task of shoveling food into his mouth.

After breakfast, Hiccup went to sit on the front step beside his grandfather, who was smoking a pipe. It was a beautiful, cold, clear winter's morning, with not a breath of wind and the sea all around as flat as glass.

Old Wrinkly blew out smoke rings contentedly as he watched the sun coming up. Hiccup shivered and chucked stones into the bracken. Neither of them spoke for a long time.

At last Hiccup said, "I got that dragon."

"I said you would, didn't I?" replied Old Wrinkly,

very pleased with himself. Old Wrinkly had taken up soothsaying in his old age, mostly unsuccessfully. Looking into the future is a complicated business. So he was particularly pleased that he'd gotten this right.

"Something extraordinary, you said," complained Hiccup. "A truly *unusual* dragon, you said. An animal that would really make me stand out in the crowd."

"Absolutely," agreed Old Wrinkly. "The entrails were undeniable."

"The *only* extraordinary thing about this dragon," continued Hiccup, "is how *extraordinarily* SMALL it is. In that it *is* super-unusual. I'm even more of a laughingstock than ever."

"Oh, dear," said Old Wrinkly, chuckling in a wheezy way over his pipe.

Hiccup looked at him reproachfully. Old Wrinkly hurriedly turned the laugh into a cough.

"Size is all relative, Hiccup," said Old Wrinkly. "ALL of these dragons are super-small compared to a real Sea Dragon. A REAL Sea Dragon is fifty *times* as big as that little creature. A real Sea Dragon from the bottom of the ocean can swallow ten large Viking ships in one gulp and not even notice.

A real Sea Dragon is a cruel, careless mystery like the mighty ocean itself, one moment calm as a scallop, the next raging like an octopus."

"Well, here on Berk," said Hiccup, "where we haven't any Sea Dragons to compare anything with, my dragon is just considerably smaller than everybody else's. You are getting off the point."

"Am I?" asked Old Wrinkly.

"The point is, I just don't see how I am ever going to become a Hero," said Hiccup gloomily. "I am the least Heroic boy in the whole Hooligan Tribe."

"Oh *pshaw,* this ridiculous Tribe," fumed Old Wrinkly. "Okay, so you are not what we call a born Hero. You're not big and tough and charismatic like Snotlout. But you're just going to have to work at it. You're going to have to learn how to be a Hero the Hard Way.

"Anyway," said Old Wrinkly, "it might be just what this Tribe needs, a change in leadership style. Because the thing is, times are changing. We can't get away with being bigger and more violent than everybody else any more. IMAGINATION. That's what they need and what you've got. A Hero of the Future is going to have to be clever and cunning, not just a big

lump with overdeveloped muscles. He's going to have
to stop everyone quarreling among themselves and get
them to face the enemy together."

"How am I going to persuade anybody to do
anything?" asked Hiccup. "They've started calling me
HICCUP THE USELESS. That is not a great name
for a Military Leader."

"You have to see the bigger picture, Hiccup,"
continued Old Wrinkly, ignoring him. "You're called
a few names. You're not a natural at Bashyball. Who
cares? These are very little problems in the grand
scheme of things."

"It's all very well for you to say they are little
problems," said Hiccup crossly, "but I have a LOT of
little problems. I have to train this super-small dragon
in time for Thor'sday Thursday or be thrown out of the
Hairy Hooligan Tribe forever."

"Ah, yes," said Old Wrinkly, thoughtfully. "There's
a book on this subject, isn't there? Remind me, how
does the great Professor of Meathead University think
you should train a dragon?"

"He thinks you should yell at it," said Hiccup,
gloomily chucking stones again. "Show the beast
who is Master by the sheer charismatic force of your

personality, that sort of thing. I have about as much charisma as a stranded jellyfish and yelling is just another thing I am useless at."

"Ye-e-es," said Old Wrinkly, "but maybe you'll have to train your dragon the Hard Way. You know a very great deal about dragons, don't you, Hiccup? All that dragon-watching you've been doing over the years?"

"That's a secret," said Hiccup, uncomfortably.

"I've seen you talking to them," said Old Wrinkly.

"That's NOT TRUE," protested Hiccup, going bright red in the face.

"Okay, then," soothed Old Wrinkly, calmly smoking his pipe, "it's not true."

There was silence for a bit.

"It *is* true," admitted Hiccup, "but for Thor's sake don't tell anybody, they wouldn't understand."

"Talking to dragons is a highly unusual skill," said Old Wrinkly. "Maybe," he said, "you can train a dragon better by talking to it than by yelling at it."

"That's sweet," said Hiccup, "and a very touching thought. However, a dragon is not a fluffy creature like a dog or a cat or a pony. A dragon is not going to do what you say just because you ask it pretty please. From what I know about dragons," said Hiccup, "I should say that yelling was a pretty good method."

"But it has its limitations, doesn't it?" Old Wrinkly pointed out. "I would say that yelling was highly effective on any dragon smaller than a sea lion. And positively suicidal if you try it on anything larger. Why don't you come up with some alternative training schemes yourself? You might be able to add something to Professor Yobbish's book. I've often thought that that book needs a little something extra . . . I can't quite put my finger on it . . ."

"WORDS," said Hiccup. "That book needs a lot more words."

6. MEANWHILE, DEEP IN THE OCEAN . . .

Meanwhile, deep in the ocean, but not so very far from the Isle of Berk, a real Sea Dragon such as Old Wrinkly had been describing lay sleeping on the sea-bed. He was indescribably large. He had been there so long that he almost seemed to be part of the ocean floor itself, a great underwater mountain, covered in shells and barnacles, some of his limbs half-buried in the sand.

Generation after generation of little hermit crabs had been born and had died in this Dragon's ears. Hundreds and hundreds of years he'd slept, because he'd had rather a large meal. He'd had the luck to catch a Roman Legion camping on a clifftop — they were completely cut off and he had spent an enjoyable afternoon wolfing down the whole lot of them, from commanding officer to lowliest private. Horses, chariots, shields, and spears, the entire lot went down the ravenous, reptilian gullet. And, while things such as golden chariot wheels are an additional source of fiber to a Dragon's diet, they do take some time to digest.

The Dragon had crawled down into the depths of the ocean and gone into a Sleep Coma. Dragons can stay in this suspended state for eternity, half-dead, half-alive, buried under fathom after fathom of icy-cold seawater. Not a muscle of this particular Dragon had moved for six or seven centuries.

But the previous week, a Killer Whale who had chased some seals unexpectedly deep was surprised to notice a slight movement in the upper eyelid of the dragon's right eye. An ancestral memory stirred in the whale's brain and he swam away from there as fast as his fins could carry him. And, a week later, the sea around the Dragon Mountain — which had previously been teeming with crabs and lobsters and shoals and shoals of fish — was a great, underwater desert. Not a mollusk stirred, not a scallop shimmied.

The only sign of life for miles and miles was the rapid jerking of both the Dragon's eyelids, fluttering up and down as if the Dragon had suddenly gone into a lighter sleep and was dreaming who knows what dark dreams.

7. TOOTHLESS WAKES UP

Toothless woke up about three weeks later. Fishlegs and Hiccup were at Hiccup's house. Everybody else was out, so Hiccup decided to take the opportunity to check on Toothless's basket. He pulled it out from under the bed. A thin plume of bluish gray smoke was drifting out from under the lid.

Fishlegs whistled. "He's awake all right," said Fishlegs. "Here we go."

Hiccup opened the basket.

The smoke billowed out and made Hiccup and Fishlegs cough. Hiccup fanned it away. Once his eyes had stopped watering he could make out a very small, ordinary dragon looking up at him with enormous, innocent, grass-green eyes.

"Hello, Toothless[1]," said Hiccup, in what he hoped was a good accent in Dragonese.

"What are you doing?" asked Fishlegs curiously. Dragonese is punctuated by shrill shrieks and popping

---

[1] This should, of course, read "Howdeedoodeethere, Toothless," but I have translated it into English for the benefit of those readers whose Dragonese is a bit rusty. Please read Hiccup's *Book 3: Learning to Speak Dragonese*, for a crash course in this fascinating language.

LEARNING TO SPEAK DRAGONESE

~INTRODUCTION~

IN ORDER TO TRAIN YOUR DRAGON WITHOUT USING THE TRADITIONAL METHODS OF YELLING AT IT, YOU MUST FIRST LEARN TO SPEAK DRAGONESE. DRAGONS ARE THE ONLY OTHER CREATURES WHO SPEAK A LANGUAGE AS COMPLICATED AND SOPHISTICATED AS HUMANS.

HERE ARE SOME COMMON DRAGON PHRASES TO GET YOU STARTED:

Nee-ah crappa inna di hoosus, pishyou.

No poo-ing inside the house, please.

≈

Mi Mama no likeit yum-yum on di bum.

My mother does not like to be
bitten on the bottom.

≈

Pishyou keendlee gobba oot mi freeundlee?

Please would you be so kind as to
spit my friend out?

≈

Doit a wummortime.

Let's try that again.

noises and sounds MOST extraordinary when spoken by a human.

"Just talking to it," mumbled Hiccup, very embarrassed.

"Just *talking* to it???" gasped Fishlegs, in astonishment. "What do you *mean*, you're talking to it? You can't talk to it, it's an ANIMAL, for Thor's sake!"

"Oh shut up, Fishlegs," said Hiccup, impatiently, "you're frightening it."

Toothless huffed and puffed and blew out some smoke rings. He inflated his neck to make himself look bigger, which is something dragons do when they are scared or angry.

Eventually he got up the courage to unfurl his wings and flap up onto Hiccup's arm. He walked his way up onto Hiccup's shoulder, and Hiccup turned his face toward him.

Toothless pressed his forehead onto Hiccup's forehead and gazed deeply and solemnly into Hiccup's eyes. They stayed there, snout to nose, without moving, for about sixty seconds. Hiccup had to blink a lot because the gaze of a dragon is hypnotic and gives the unnerving feeling that it is sucking your soul away.

Hiccup was just thinking, "Wow, this is amazing —

I'm really making contact here!" when Toothless bent down and bit him on the arm.

Hiccup let out a yelp and threw Toothless off him. "F-f-fish," hissed Toothless, hovering in the air in front of Hiccup. "W-w-w-want fish NOW!"

"I haven't got any fish," said Hiccup in Dragonese, rubbing his arm. Luckily Toothless didn't have any teeth, but dragons have powerful jaws so it was still painful. Toothless bit him on the other arm. "F-F-F-FISH!" said Toothless again.

"Are you okay?" asked Fishlegs. "I can't believe I'm asking this, but what's he saying?"

"He wants to eat," replied Hiccup, grimly rubbing both arms. He tried to make his voice sound firm but pleasant; to dominate the creature by the sheer force of his personality, as Gobber had said. "But WE HAVE NO FISH."

"Okay then," said Toothless. "Eat c-c-cat."

He made a lunge for Fiddlesticks, who streaked up the nearest wall with a yowl of terror.

Hiccup just managed to grab Toothless by the tail as he flew off in pursuit. The dragon struggled wildly, shouting "WANT F-F-FISH NOW! WANT F-F-FOOD NOW! CATS ARE YUMMY WANT FOOD NOW!"

"We don't HAVE any fish," repeated Hiccup, from between gritted teeth, feeling all his calmness deserting him, "and you can't eat the cat — I like him."

Fiddlesticks mewed indignantly from a beam high up in the roof.

They put Toothless in Stoick's bedroom, where there was a mouse problem.

For a while he was happy swooping after the desperately squeaking mice, but then he got bored and started attacking the mattress.

"STOP!" yelled Hiccup as feathers flew in all directions.

Toothless replied by throwing up the remains of a recently deceased mouse right in the middle of Stoick's pillow.

"Aaaargh!" said Hiccup.

"AAAAAAARGH!" said Stoick the Vast, who entered the room at that very moment.

Toothless launched himself at Stoick the Vast's beard, which he mistook for a chicken.

"Get him off!" said Stoick.

"He doesn't do what I say," said Hiccup.

"Yell VERY LOUDLY at him," Stoick shouted, VERY LOUDLY.

Hiccup yelled as loudly as he could. "Please will you stop eating my father's beard?"

As Hiccup had suspected, Toothless took absolutely no notice whatsoever.

I KNEW I'd be useless at yelling, thought Hiccup gloomily.

"DROPTOTHEFLOORYOUORRRIBLELIT-TLEREPTILE!" yelled Stoick.

Toothless dropped to the floor.

"You see?" said Stoick. "*That's* how to deal with dragons."

Newtsbreath and Hookfang, Stoick's hunting dragons, came padding into the room. Toothless stiffened as they paced around him, their yellow eyes glinting evilly. Each was about the size of a leopard, and they were as delighted by his arrival as a couple of giant cats might be by that of a cute little kitten.

"Greetings, fellow firebreather," hissed Newtsbreath as he gave the wriggling newcomer a sniff.

"We must wait," purred Hookfang menacingly, "until we are alone and then we can give you a proper welcome." He gave a vicious swipe at Toothless with one paw. A claw like a kitchen knife just nicked Toothless on the rump and the little dragon howled and jumped into Hiccup's tunic, until only his tail was poking out of the neck.

"HOOKFANG!" bellowed Stoick.

"My claw slipped," whined Hookfang.

"GEDDOUTOFHEREBEFOREIMAKEYOUIN-TOHANDBAGS!" yelled Stoick, and Newtsbreath and Hookfang slunk out, muttering obscene dragon curses under their breaths.

"As I was saying," said Stoick the Vast. "THAT'S how to deal with dragons."

Stoick was looking at Toothless with uncharacteristic anxiety.

"Son," said Stoick, hoping there might be some sort of mistake, "is this dragon *your* dragon?"

"Yes, father," Hiccup admitted.

"It's very . . . well . . . it's very . . . SMALL, isn't it?" said Stoick slowly.

Stoick was not an observant person but even *he* could not fail to notice that this dragon really *was* remarkably small.

". . . and it hasn't got any teeth."

There was an awkward silence.

Fishlegs came to Hiccup's rescue.

"That's because it's an unusual breed," said Fishlegs. "A unique and . . . er . . . violent species called the Toothless Daydream, distant relations of the

Monstrous Nightmare, but far more ruthless and so rare they are practically extinct."

"Really?" Stoick surveyed the Toothless Daydream doubtfully. "It looks just like a Common or Garden to me."

"Ahhh, but with respect, Chief," said Fishlegs, "that's where you're WRONG. To the amateur eye and, indeed, to its prey, it looks *exactly* like a Common or Garden. But if you look a little closer the characteristic Daydream marking" — Fishlegs pointed to a wart on the end of Toothless's nose — "marks it out from the more ordinary breed."

"By Thor, you're right!" said Stoick.

"And it's not just your *average* Toothless Daydream either." Fishlegs was getting carried away now. "This particular dragon is of ROYAL BLOOD."

"No!" said Stoick, very impressed. Stoick was a terrific snob.

"Yes," said Fishlegs solemnly. "Your son has only gone and burgled the offspring of King Daggerfangs himself, the reptilian ruler of Wild Dragon Cliff. The Royal Daydreams tend to start out small but they grow into creatures of IMPRESSIVE — even GARGANTUAN — size."

"Just like you, eh, Hiccup," said Stoick, giving a great laugh and ruffling his son's hair.

Stoick's tummy gave out a plaintive rumble like a distant underground explosion. "Time for a little supper, I think. Clear up this mess, will you, boys?"

Stoick strode off, relieved to have had his faith in his son restored.

"Thanks, Fishlegs," said Hiccup. "You were inspired."

"Not at all," said Fishlegs. "I owed you one after setting you up for that fight with Snotlout."

"Father's going to find out at some point anyway, though," said Hiccup gloomily.

"Not necessarily," said Fishlegs. "Look at all that talking you were doing with the Toothless Daydream here. That was INCREDIBLE. UNBELIEVABLE. I've never seen anything like it. You'll be training him in next to no time."

"I was talking to him, all right," said Hiccup, "but he didn't listen to a word I said."

♦ ♦ ♦

When he was going to bed that night, Hiccup didn't want to leave Toothless in front of the fire with Newtsbreath and Hookfang.

"Can I take him to bed with me?" he asked Stoick.

"A dragon is a working animal," said Stoick the Vast. "Too much hugging and kissing will make him lose his vicious streak."

"But Newtsbreath will kill him if I leave him alone with them."

Newtsbreath gave an appreciative growl. "It would be my pleasure," he hissed.

"Nonsense," boomed Stoick, unaware of Newtsbreath's last remark, as he didn't speak Dragonese. He gave Newtsbreath a friendly cuff round the horns. "Newtsbreath just wants to play. That sort of rough-and-tumble is good for a young dragon. Makes him learn to stick up for himself."

Hookfang extended his claws like switchblades and drummed them on the hearth.

Hiccup pretended to say goodnight to Toothless by the fire, but smuggled him into the bedroom under his tunic.

"You must be absolutely quiet," he told Toothless sternly as they climbed into bed, and the dragon nodded eagerly. In fact, he snored loudly the entire night, but Hiccup didn't care. Hiccup spent the whole of the winter on Berk in various states of "very cold," ranging from "fairly chilly" to "absolutely freezing." At night, too many layers were considered sissy, so Hiccup generally lay awake for a couple of hours until he had shivered himself into a light sleep.

Now, though, as Hiccup stretched his feet out against Toothless's back, he felt waves of heat coming off the little dragon, gradually creeping up his legs and warming his freezing cold stomach and heart, even traveling right up to his head, which hadn't been *truly* warm for almost six months. Even his ears burned contentedly. It would have taken the snoring of six strong dragons to have woken Hiccup, so deeply did he sleep that night.

8. TRAINING YOUR DRAGON THE HARD WAY

Hiccup was still pretty certain, knowing dragons as he did, that yelling was the easiest method of training them. So, over the next couple of weeks, he tried yelling at Toothless to see if he could make it work. He tried yelling loudly, firmly, strictly. He looked as cross as he could. But Toothless wouldn't take him seriously.

Hiccup finally gave up on the yelling when Toothless stole a kipper off his plate one morning at breakfast. Hiccup let out his most fierce and frightening yell and Toothless just gave him a wicked look and knocked everything else on to the floor with one swipe of his tail.

That was it with the yelling, as far as Hiccup was concerned.

"Okay, then," said Hiccup, "I'll try going to the other extreme."

So he was as nice to Toothless as he possibly could be. He gave Toothless the comfiest bit of the bed and lay dangerously balanced on the edge of it himself.

He fed him as much kipper and lobster as he wanted. He only did this once, though, as the little dragon just went on eating until he had made himself thoroughly sick.

He played games with him for hours and hours. He told him jokes, he brought him mice to eat, he scratched the bit that Toothless couldn't quite reach in between the spokes on his back.

He made that dragon's life as close to Dragon Heaven as he possibly could.

♥ ♥ ♥

By mid February, the winter was coming to an end on Berk, and the snowy season had turned into the rainy season. It was the kind of weather where your clothes never got dry, no matter what. Hiccup would hang up his sodden tunic on a chair in front of the fire before going to bed at night, and in the morning it would *still* be wet — warm and wet rather than cold and wet, but WET nonetheless.

The ground all around the Village had turned into knee-deep mud.

"What, in Woden's name, are you doing?" asked Fishlegs when he came across Hiccup digging a large hole just outside the house.

"Building a mud wallow for Toothless," panted Hiccup.

"You spoil that dragon, you really do," said Fishlegs, shaking his head.

"It's psychology, you see," said Hiccup. "It's clever and it's subtle, not like that caveman yelling you're doing with Horrorcow."

Fishlegs had named his dragon Horrorcow. The "horror" bit was to make the poor creature at least sound a bit frightening. The "cow" bit was because for a dragon she really *was* remarkably like a cow. She was a large, peaceful, brown creature, with an easy-going nature. Fishlegs suspected she might even be vegetarian.

"I'm always catching her nibbling at the woodwork," he complained. "BLOOD, Horrorcow, BLOOD — that's what you should want!"

Nonetheless, maybe Fishlegs *was* a better yeller than Hiccup, or maybe Horrorcow was a lazier and more obliging character than Toothless, but Horrorcow was proving very easy to train by the yelling method.

"Okay, Toothless, it's ready," said Hiccup. "Get yourself a good wallow."

Toothless stopped trying to catch voles and

leaped into the mud. He rolled over and over in the oozy muck, spreading out his wings and squirming happily.

"I'm bonding with him," said Hiccup, "so he'll want to do what I say."

"Hiccup," said Fishlegs, as Toothless sucked up a good mouthful of the mud and spat it out straight into Hiccup's face, "I may not know much about dragons, but I *do* know that they are the most selfish creatures on Earth. No dragon is ever going to do what you want out of gratitude. Dragons do not know what gratitude is. Give up. This will NEVER WORK."

"The thing about us d-d-dragons," said Toothless, helpfully, "is we're s-s-survivors. We're not like s-s-sappy cats or d-d-dumb dogs, falling in l-l-love with their Masters and yucky things like that.

Only reason we ever do what a m-m-man wants is because he's b-b-bigger than us and gives us food."

"What's he saying?" asked Fishlegs.

"Pretty much what you're saying," said Hiccup.

"N-n-never trust a dragon," said Toothless, cheerfully hopping out of the wallow and helping himself to one of the winkles that Hiccup had found for him (Toothless was particularly fond of winkles — "J-j-just like picking your n-n-nose," he had said). "That's what my m-m-mother taught me in the nest, and she should know."

Hiccup sighed. It was true. Toothless was cute to look at, and very good company — if a little demanding. However, you only had to look into his big, innocent, heavily lashed eyes to realize that he was totally without morals. The eyes were ancient, the eyes of a killer. You might as well ask a crocodile or a shark to be your friend.

Hiccup wiped the mud off his face.

"I'll think of something else," said Hiccup.

❤ ❤ ❤

February turned into March and Hiccup was still thinking. A few flowers made the mistake of appearing and were immediately blasted out of existence by a couple of hard frosts that had kept themselves back for this very purpose.

Fishlegs could now get Horrorcow to "go" and "stay" on command. Hiccup was still struggling to teach Toothless the basics of toilet training.

"NO POOING IN THE KITCHEN," said Hiccup for the hundredth time, carrying Toothless outside after yet another accident.

"Is w-w-warmer in the kitchen," whined Toothless.

"But poos go OUTSIDE, you KNOW that," said Hiccup, at the end of his tether.

Toothless promptly pooed all over Hiccup's hands and down his tunic.

"Is OUTSIDE, is OUTSIDE, is OUTSIDE," crowed Toothless.

At this inopportune moment, Snotlout and Dogsbreath came sauntering past Stoick's house on the way back from the beach, their dragons on their shoulders.

"Well, well, well," sneered Snotlout, "if it isn't the USELESS, covered in dragon poo. It actually quite suits you."

"Hur, Hur, Hur," snorted Dogsbreath.

"That's not a dragon," jeered Seaslug, Dogsbreath's dragon, who was an ugly great Gronckle with a pug nose and a mean temper, "that's a newt with wings."

SEASLUG

"That's not a dragon," scoffed Fireworm, Snotlout's dragon, who was as big a bully as her master, "that's an ickle newborn bunny wabbit with a pathetic poo problem."

Toothless gave a gasp of fury.

Snotlout showed Hiccup the immense heap of fish that he had wrapped up in his cloak.

"Look what Fireworm and Seaslug caught down at the beach. And it only took a couple of hours. . . ."

Fireworm coughed, flexed a shining muscle or two, and looked at her claws in fake modesty. "Oh, please," she drawled. "I wasn't even CONCENTRATING. If I was TRYING, I could do it in ten minutes, with one wing tied behind my back."

"Excuse me while I throw up," muttered Toothless to Horrorcow, who was regarding Fireworm with disapproval in her big brown eyes.

Fireworm

"We reckon Fireworm could be a bit of a HUNTING LEGEND," grinned Snotlout. "I hear that Horrorcow is partial to carrots. . . . Has the Toothless Wonder gotten up the nerve to attack a vegetable? Carrots are a bit crunchy but perhaps he could manage the odd squished cucumber. . . . You could give it to him through a straw perhaps. . . ."

"HUR, HUR, HUR." Dogsbreath laughed so hard that snot came snorting out of his nose.

"Careful, Dogsbreath," said Fishlegs politely, "your brains are coming out."

Dogsbreath bashed him hard and the two boys staggered off, Fireworm making a lunge at Toothless that nearly took his eye out as he went past.

As soon as they were safely out of earshot, Toothless jumped out of Hiccup's arms and coughed out sheets of flame in a menacing manner.

"Bullies! Yellowbellies! Come closer and Toothless'll fry you to a frazzle! Toothless'll drag out yer guts and play 'em on a harp! Toothless'll . . . Toothless'll . . . Toothless'll . . . well, you just better not come any closer, that's all . . . !"

"Oh, very brave, Toothless," said Hiccup sarcastically. "If you shout louder they might even hear you."

9. FEAR, VANITY, REVENGE, AND SILLY JOKES

March turned into April and April turned into May. After Fireworm's remark about the pathetic bunny rabbit, Toothless never pooed in the kitchen again. But Hiccup hadn't made any further progress in training him.

It was still raining, but it was a warm rain. The wind was blowing, but it was a less furious wind. It was just about possible to stand upright.

The gulls' eggs were hatching on the rocks and the parent gulls dive-bombed Hiccup and Fishlegs when they came to the Long Beach to practice.

"KILL, Horrorcow, KILL," said Fishlegs to Horrorcow, who was calmly perched on his shoulder. "You could have that Black-backed Gull for breakfast, he's barely half your size. Honestly, Hiccup, I give up, I don't know how I'm going to pass the hunting section of the test, Horrorcow just doesn't have the killer instinct. She'd never survive in the wild."

Hiccup laughed hollowly. "You think YOU'VE got problems? Toothless and I are failing right from the beginning: the basic obedience commands, the retrieval, the compulsory exercises, the hunting — the lot."

"It can't be *that* bad," said Fishlegs.

"Watch," said Hiccup.

The boys moved along the beach a bit, out of range of the gulls.

They started practicing the most basic command of all: "go." The dragon was supposed to stand, bolt upright, on the handler's outstretched arm. The handler would then bark the command as loudly as possible while simultaneously lifting his arm to fling the dragon into the air. The dragon was supposed to soar gracefully into flight when the handler's arm reached its highest point.

Horrorcow yawned, scratched, and slowly flapped off, grumbling to herself.

Toothless was even less obedient.

"GO!" yelled Hiccup.

Hiccup flung his arm up. Toothless hung on.

"I said GO!" Hiccup repeated in frustration.

"W-w-why g-g-go?" shuddered Toothless, gripping even tighter.

Toothless would not budge...

"Just go GO GO GO GO!!!!" screamed Hiccup, flapping his arm up and down frantically, with Toothless hanging on to it for dear life.

Toothless stayed.

"Toothless," said Hiccup, as reasonably as he could, "please go. If you don't start going when I tell you to, we are both going to be thrown into exile."

"But I don't w-w-want to go," Toothless pointed out, equally reasonably.

Fishlegs watched the whole process in appalled amazement. "You really *do* have problems," he said in an awed voice.

"Yup," said Hiccup. He finally managed to uncurl Toothless's claws, which had relaxed their grip for a second, and pushed him off. Toothless landed on the sand with a squeal of outrage, and immediately attached himself to Hiccup's leg, getting a good grip on the sandals with his talons, and wrapping his wings around Hiccup's calf.

"N-n-not going," said Toothless stubbornly.

"It can't get much worse than this," said Hiccup, "so I'm going to try a new tack."

He took out the notebook in which he had been jotting down all he knew about dragons in the hope that it might be useful. "DRAGON MOTIVATION . . ." Hiccup read aloud, "Number one. GRATITUDE." Hiccup sighed. "Number two. FEAR. That works, but I can't do it. Three, four, five: GREED, VANITY, and REVENGE. Those are all worth a try. Six. JOKES AND RIDDLING TALK. Only if I'm desperate."

"This has got to be a first," drawled Fishlegs, "but

Hiccup

DRAGON MOTIVASHUN

1. ~~GRATITUDE~~ Dragons are never~~st~~ grateful

2. ~~FEAR~~. Works but I cant do it.

3. ~~GREED~~ cood fill him up so much he can't fly ?

4. VANITTY. Possible.

5. Revenge ??? Worth a try

6. JOKES AND RIDDLING TALK.
↑
only if Im desparate.

THE MONSTROUS NIGHTMARE

The Monstrous Nightmare is the largest and most terrifying of the domestic dragons. Dazzling flyers, magnificent hunters, and fearsome fighters, they can be wild and difficult to train. By unofficial Viking Law, only a Chief or the son of a Chief can own one.

~ STATISTICS ~

COLORS: Emerald green, brilliant scarlet, deepest purple.

ARMED WITH: Scary fangs, extra-extendable claws **9**

DEFENSES: Nightmares don't need defenses **2**

RADAR: None **0**

POISON: Bite is slightly poisonous **3**

HUNTING ABILITY: Amazing to watch **10**

SPEED: Fast **7**

FEAR AND FIGHT FACTOR: Very, very scary **10**

I'm with Gobber the Belch on this one. Why don't you just yell a bit louder?"

Hiccup ignored him.

"Okay, Toothless," said Hiccup to the little dragon, who was pretending to be asleep as he held on to Hiccup's leg. "For every fish you catch me I will give you two more lobsters when you get home."

Toothless opened his eyes. "A-a-alive?" he said eagerly. "C-c-can Toothless kill them? P-p-please? Just this once?"

"No, Toothless," said Hiccup, firmly, "I keep on telling you, it isn't kind to torture creatures smaller than yourself."

Toothless closed his eyes again. "You're so b-b-boring," he said sulkily.

"You're such a clever, quick dragon, Toothless," Hiccup flattered, "I bet you could catch more fish than any of the others on Thor'sday Thursday if you wanted to."

Toothless opened his eyes to consider the matter. "T-t-twice as many," he said modestly. "But I don't w-w-want to."

This was unanswerable. Hiccup crossed VANITY off his list.

"You know that big red Fireworm dragon who was so rude to you?" said Hiccup.

Toothless spat on the ground in indignation. "S-s-said I was a newt with wings. S-s-said I was an incontinent bunny r-r-rabbit. T-t-toothless going to k-k-kill her. Toothless going to s-s-scratch her to death. T-t-toothless going to —"

"Yes, yes, yes," said Hiccup hastily. "That Fireworm dragon and her master who looks like a pig think that Fireworm is going to catch more fish than anybody else at the Thor'sday Thursday celebrations. Think how stupid they are going to look if YOU win the prize for Most Promising Dragon instead of her."

Toothless got off Hiccup's leg. "I W-W-WILL think about that," said Toothless. He waddled off a couple of feet and thought about it.

Five minutes later he was still thinking. He let out the odd chuckle every now and then, but every time Hiccup said, "So, how about it, then?" he just replied, "S-s-still thinking. Go away."

With a sigh, Hiccup put a line through REVENGE.

"Okay," said Fishlegs, looking over Hiccup's shoulder. "You've tried everything else. How about

JOKES AND RIDDLING TALK? I assume you're desperate."

"Toothless," said Hiccup, "If you catch me a nice big mackerel you will be the cleverest, fastest dragon on Berk AND you will make that Fireworm dragon look like an idiot AND you will have all the lobsters you can eat when we get home AND I will tell you a really good joke."

Toothless turned around. "T-t-toothless loves jokes." He flapped on to Hiccup's arm again. "All right. Toothless help you. B-b-but NOT because me being n-n-nice or anything yucky. . . ."

"No, no," said Hiccup. "Of course not."

"Us d-d-dragons cruel and mean. But we do love a j-j-joke. Tell me NOW."

Hiccup laughed. "No way. AFTER you bring me a mackerel."

"Okay, then," said Toothless. He jumped off Hiccup's arm into the air.

A dragon hunting is a very impressive sight, even a scrawny infant one like Toothless. He flew across the beach in his usual untidy, lopsided fashion, shrieking a few insults along the way at any cormorants that looked smaller than him. But as soon as he reached the sea, Toothless seemed to grow up a bit. The sea-salt awoke in him some ancestral memory of the great pedigree hunting monsters that were his forefathers. He spread out his wings like a kite and flew fairly swiftly over the surface of the choppy waves, keeping his body and wings steady as he searched for the movement of fish. He spotted something, and soared upward in circles until he was so high that Hiccup, craning his neck backward on the beach, could only just see him as a tiny speck. The speck was motionless for a second, and then Toothless dived, his wings folded by his sides, dropping like a stone out of the sky.

He disappeared into the water and was gone for quite a while. Dragons can stay under water for at least five minutes, if they want to, and Toothless got quite distracted under there, chasing one fish and then another, unable to decide which was the biggest.

Hiccup had gotten bored and was looking for oysters when Toothless came bursting triumphantly out of the sea carrying a small mackerel.

He dropped the mackerel at Hiccup's feet, did three somersaults in a row, and landed on Hiccup's head. He let out the dragon's cry of triumph, which is a bit like a rooster

crowing but a lot louder and more
self-satisfied.

Then he leaned over and stared
into Hiccup's eyes, upside down.

"Now t-t-tell me a joke," said Toothless.

"Whimpering Wodens," said Hiccup. "He did it.
He really did it."

"T-t-tell me a JOKE," said Toothless again.

"What's black and white and red all over?"
asked Hiccup.

Toothless didn't know.

"A sunburned penguin," replied Hiccup.

It was a very, very old joke, but apparently it
hadn't made it to Wild Dragon Cliff. Toothless thought
it was hysterically funny.

He flew off to catch more fish so he could hear
more jokes.

It was an enjoyable afternoon. The rain stopped,
the sun shone, and Toothless didn't do too badly at all
with the hunting. He dropped a few fish and, at one
point, wandered off entirely to chase rabbits on the
clifftops. But he came back when Hiccup called,
eventually, and by the end of a couple of hours he had
caught six medium-sized mackerel and a dogfish.

All in all, Hiccup was pretty satisfied.

"After all," he said to Fishlegs, "it's not like I'm expecting to win the prize for Most Promising Dragon or anything. All I need is to show that Toothless is basically under my control and for him to catch a few fish. We'll make fools of ourselves compared to Snotlout and his beastly Hunting Legend, but at least we'll have passed Initiation."

What was more, as Toothless dropped the last mackerel on the heap in front of Hiccup, Fishlegs noticed something sharp and gleaming in the dragon's lower jaw.

"Toothless has gotten his first tooth!" said Fishlegs. It seemed a very good omen.

♥ ♥ ♥

As they staggered home they passed Old Wrinkly, who had been sitting on a rock watching them for the past couple of hours.

"Ve-ry impressive," wheezed Old Wrinkly as the boys showed him the fish wrapped up in Hiccup's cloak.

"We reckon Hiccup really might pass the Final Initiation Test on Thor'sday Thursday," said Fishlegs excitedly.

"So you're still worrying about that piddly little Test, are you, Hiccup?" asked Old Wrinkly. "There are larger concerns, you know. There's a gi-normous storm brewing up, for instance. It should hit us in about three days."

"Piddly little Test?" said Fishlegs indignantly. "What do you mean, piddly little Test??? The Thor'sday Thursday Festival is the biggest event of the year. EVERYBODY who is ANYBODY will be there, all the Hairy Hooligans AND the Meatheads. Plus, this may not seem important to YOU, but anybody who fails this piddly little Test gets put into exile to get eaten up by cannibals or something equally gruesome."

"I'm going to call myself HICCUP THE USEFUL and his dragon TOOTHFULL," said Hiccup, beaming. "I thought of it just now and I'm really pleased with it. It's solid, dependable, not too flashy and not too much to live up to."

"This reptile finally got his act together and caught some fish," said Fishlegs, pointing at Toothless, who was picking his nose with one claw. "Incredible though it may seem, Hiccup may pass this Test after all."

"Oh, I think it's almost a certainty," said Old Wrinkly, looking at Toothless, who was now attempting to cross his eyes and was falling down in the process.

"Al-most," repeated Old Wrinkly thoughtfully.

And the boys went home, with Toothless following behind them whining, "Oh C-C-CARRY ME, CARRY ME . . . it's not f-f-fair . . . my wings ache. . . ."

Toothless

10. THOR'SDAY THURSDAY

The Thor'sday Thursday Celebrations were a truly
spectacular occasion. The Hairy Hooligans' fierce ri-
vals, the Meatheads, from the nearby Meathead
Islands, sailed across the Inner Ocean to the Isle of
Berk for this great gathering.

The visitors set up camp in Black Heart Bay,
which turned overnight from an empty desert of echoing seagulls into a bustling village of tents made out of
sails too patched to be used at sea anymore.

By the next morning the Long Beach was
packed with stalls and jugglers and fortune tellers.
There was a happy confusion of Vikings spotting old
friends, and practicing their sword play, and yelling at
the children to stop hitting each other RIGHT NOW
for Thor's sake no I REALLY MEAN IT this time . . .
or . . . or . . . or . . . ELSE.

Vast Viking men sat on uncomfortable rocks

WELCOME TO THE
THOR'SDAY THURSDAY CELEBRATION!

– – – –

Program of events

– – – –

9:00 Hammer-throwing for the Over-60s only.
Meet up at the Marooner's Rock with your own hammer or somebody else's (hard hats essential for spectators).

–

10:30 How Many Gulls' Eggs Can You Eat in One Minute?
Baggybum the Beerbelly is the defending champion in this hotly contested competition.

–

11:30 Ugliest Baby Contest

–

12:30 Axe-fighting Display
Admire the delicate art of fighting with axes.

–

2:00 Young Heroes Final Initiation Test
Watch tomorrow's Viking Heroes as they compete. Whose dragon will be the most obedient, and whose will catch the most fish? Blood, teeth, loud yelling – this sport has everything.

–

3:30 Grand Raffle and Closing Ceremony

guffawing loudly like gigantic sea lions in a holiday mood. Impressively large Viking women huddled in groups cackling like seagulls and downing whole mugs of tea in one swallow.

Despite Old Wrinkly's gloomy forecasts of terrible storms and typhoons, it was a gloriously hot June day with not even a hint of a cloud in the offing.

The Young Heroes Final Initiation Test would not start until 2 P.M. that afternoon, so Hiccup spent the morning listening round-eyed to storytellers telling tall tales of Dirty Danes and pirate princesses.

He was sick with nerves, so he found it difficult to enjoy the occasion as much as he had in previous years.

Even Gobber throwing up during the How Many Gulls' Eggs Can You Eat in One Minute? competition failed to raise more than a faint smile on his pale, tense face.

Hiccup's family had a picnic lunch overlooking the Axe-fighting Display. Hiccup could not eat a thing, and nor, unusually, could Toothless, who was in a difficult mood and turned his nose up at the tuna sandwich Valhallarama offered.

"Good to keep your dragon's appetite sharp for the game," boomed Stoick the Vast, who was in an excellent mood. He had won a bet on Goggletoad in the Ugliest Baby Contest and was looking forward to seeing his son's brilliant display during the Initiation Test.

As the day wore on, a hot wind suddenly started blowing out of nowhere. It was still sweltering, but ominous gray clouds were gathering on the horizon. There was the odd rumble of thunder in the air.

Maybe Old Wrinkly had been right, thought Hiccup as he gazed upward, *and Thor* is *going to put in his traditional appearance at the Thor'sday Thursday celebrations.*

"P-P-P-P-A-R-P! Will all youths hoping to be initiated into the Tribes this year please make their way to the ground at the left of the beach."

Hiccup gulped, nudged Toothless, and stood up. This was it.

♥ ♥ ♥

Hiccup was one of the last to get to the ground, which was a large area of wet sand just at the edge of the sea. The boys from his own Tribe were already assembled, their dragons hovering a couple of feet above them.

Everybody was chattering excitedly, and even Snotlout was looking nervous.

The Meathead boys and their dragons seemed to be gigantic, rough-looking customers, far tougher than the Hooligans. One in particular was a great hulking brute of a boy, who looked fifteen at least.

Thuggory the Meathead and his dragon
KILLER

Hiccup presumed he was Thuggory, Chief Mogadon the Meathead's son, because a silver-gray Monstrous Nightmare about three feet tall was perched on one of his shoulders. It was looking at Fireworm like a rottweiler thinking evil thoughts.

Fireworm acted unconcerned.

"An aristocrat never growls," purred Fireworm sweetly. "You must be one of those mongrel Nightmares. We pure greenbloods descended from the great Ripperclaw himself would never *dream* of doing anything so common."

The silver Nightmare's growling increased in volume.

The crowd was assembling at the touchline. Hiccup tried not to notice Stoick the Vast blasting his way to the front with great cries of, "Out of my way, I'm a CHIEF."

"TEN TO ONE MY SON CATCHES MORE FISH THAN YOUR SON IN THIS TEST," boomed Stoick, giving his old enemy Mogadon the Meathead a good prod in the stomach.

Mogadon the Meathead narrowed his eyes and wondered whether to hit him. Maybe AFTER the Test.

"And which," asked Mogadon the Meathead, "is

your son? Is he the tall one who looks like a pig with the skeleton tattoos and the red Monstrous Nightmare?"

"Nope," said Stoick happily. "That's my brother Baggybum's son. **MY SON** is that skinny one over there with the Toothless Daydream."

Mogadon the Meathead broke into a big smile.

He slapped Stoick, on the back and yelled, "I TAKE YOUR BET AND DOUBLE IT!"

"DONE!" shouted Stoick, and the two great chieftains shook hands and bumped bellies on the bet.

♦ ♦ ♦

Gobber the Belch was in charge of this final stage of the Initiation Test. He was still looking a bit green from his unpleasant experience in the How Many Gulls' Eggs Can You Eat in One Minute? competition. This had not improved his temper.

"ALL RIGHT, YOU 'ORRIBLE LOT!" yelled Gobber. "This is where we find out if you are the stuff that Heroes are made of. You will either walk out of this arena full members of the noble Tribes of Hairy

Hooligans and Merciless Meatheads OR go into miserable exile forever from the Inner Isles. Let's see which it's going to be, shall we?"

He grinned nastily at the twenty boys standing before him.

"I shall begin by inspecting you and your animals, as if you were warriors about to go into battle. I shall introduce you to the watching members of the Tribes you hope to enter. Then the Test will begin. You will demonstrate how you have asserted yourselves over these wild creatures and tamed them by the sheer force of your Heroic Personalities.

"You will start by performing the basic commands of 'go,' 'stay,' and 'fetch.' You will end by ordering your reptile to hunt fish for you, as your forefathers have done before you."

Hiccup swallowed nervously.

"The boy and dragon who most impress the judge, and that is ME," — Gobber bared his teeth grimly — "will receive the extra glory of being called the Hero of Heroes and Most Promising Dragon. The boys and dragons who FAIL this Test will say farewell to their families forever and leave the Tribe to go, where we do not care." Gobber paused.

"Poetry," muttered Fishlegs, just loud enough for Gobber to hear. Gobber glared at him.

"HEROES OR EXILES!" yelled Gobber the Belch.

"HEROES OR EXILES!" yelled eighteen boys fanatically back at him.

"HEROES OR EXILES!" yelled the watching Hooligan and Meathead Tribes.

Please let me be a bit of a Hero, just this once, Hiccup and Fishlegs each thought to themselves. Nothing too spectacular or anything, just to get through this Test.

"STAND TO ATTENTION, WITH YOUR DRAGONS ON YOUR RIGHT ARMS!" yelled Gobber the Belch.

Gobber walked down the row of boys for the inspection.

"Beautiful turnout." Gobber congratulated Thuggory the Meathead on his Nightmare dragon, Killer, who spread out his shining wings to show off a wingspan of about four feet.

Gobber stopped abruptly when he got to Hiccup.

"And WHAT in the name of Woden," demanded Gobber, blanching a little, "is THIS?"

"It's a Toothless Daydream, sir," muttered Hiccup.

"Small but vicious," added Fishlegs, helpfully.

"Toothless Daydream???" blustered Gobber. "That's the smallest Common or Garden I have ever seen. What do you think I am, an idiot?"

"No, no, sir," murmured Fishlegs reassuringly, "just a little on the slow side."

Gobber glowered dangerously.

"A Toothless Daydream," explained Hiccup, "looks exactly like a Common or Garden except for the characteristic wart on the end of its nose."

"SILENCE!" said Gobber, in a very loud whisper. "Or I shall throw you all the way to the Mainland. I HOPE," he continued, "that this dragon hunts better than it looks. You and your fishy friend here are the worst candidates for Initiation I have ever had the displeasure of teaching. But you are the future of this Tribe, Hiccup, and if you shame us in front of the Meatheads, I, personally, will never forgive you. Do you understand?"

Hiccup nodded.

Each boy then stepped forward to bow and hold up his dragon for the spectators to applaud.

There was huge clapping for Snotface Snotlout and his dragon, Fireworm, rivaled only by the mighty cheering for Thuggory the Meathead and his dragon, Killer.

"I give you, last but not least," Gobber the Belch was trying to put a bit of enthusiasm into his yelling, "the fearsome . . . the terrible . . . the only son of Stoick the Vast . . . HICCUP THE USEFUL AND HIS DRAGON TOOTHFULL!"

Hiccup stepped forward and held up Toothless as high as he could to make him look a bit bigger.

There was a slightly appalled silence.

People had seen dragons this small before, of course, normally scampering about after field mice in the wild, but NOT as noble hunting dragons competing in Initiation.

"SIZE ISN'T EVERYTHING!" boomed Stoick, so loudly that you could have heard him several beaches away, and he banged his great hands together to start the applause.

Everyone was terrified of Stoick's famous temper, so they joined in with polite wild cheering.

Toothless was still in a mood, but he was

delighted to be the center of attention, and he puffed out his chest and bowed solemnly to left and right.

A few of the Meatheads snickered.

I've changed my mind, thought Hiccup, closing his eyes, *THIS is the worst moment of my life so far.*

"Okay, Toothless," he whispered into the little dragon's ear, "this is our Big Chance. Catch lots of fish here and I will tell you more jokes than you have ever heard in your life. Which will make that big red Fireworm dragon *really* cross."

Toothless took a sideways glance at Fireworm. She was sharpening her nails on Snotlout's helmet with the smug certainty of a dragon who knows she's about to win the prize for Most Promising Dragon.

"P-P-PARP!"

The Test began.

♦ ♦ ♦

Toothless didn't do too badly in the early obedience exercises, though he clearly thought it was extremely dull. It was now raining quite hard and Toothless hated the rain. He wanted to go home and relax in front of a nice warm fire.

Fireworm and Killer were "going" and "fetching" as soon as Snotlout and Thuggory commanded, and they were diving and breathing out fire as they did so, just to show off. Fireworm did some fancy acrobatic somersaults that had the crowd screaming and stamping their feet.

"START YOUR HUNTING!" yelled Gobber the Belch.

Every dragon except Toothless flew out to sea.

Toothless flapped back to Hiccup's shoulder.

"T-T-Toothless got a t-t-tummy-ache," he complained. Hiccup tried not to see his father looking surprised on the sidelines.

He tried not to notice the crowd whispering to each other: "That's Stoick's son over there — no, not the tall one with the skeleton tattoos who looks like a pig, the small skinny one who can't even control his minuscule dragon."

Toothless got a tummy-ache.

"Don't forget, Toothless," said Hiccup through gritted teeth, "the FISH. I'm going to tell you all the jokes I've ever heard, remember?"

"T-t-tell me NOW," said Toothless.

Help came from an unexpected quarter.

Snotlout broke off from yelling "KILL, FIREWORM, KILL" to lean over and sneer at Hiccup. "What ARE you doing, Hiccup? You're not TALKING to that newt with wings, are you? Talking to dragons is against the rules and forbidden by order of Stoick the Vast, your wimpy father. . . ."

"N-n-newt with wings?" repeated Toothless. "N-N-NEWT WITH WINGS???"

"You're not a newt with wings, are you, Toothless?" said Hiccup. "You're the best hunter in the world, aren't you?"

"Too RIGHT I am," said Toothless, grumpily.

"You SHOW that Snotface Snotlout and his snobby dragon what a REAL hunting dragon can do," said Hiccup urgently.

"OKAY, then," said Toothless.

Hiccup heaved a huge sigh of relief as Toothless took off in shambolic fashion in the general direction of the sea.

"This is too good to be true," Hiccup said to himself ten minutes later as Toothless returned from a second trip, clearly too bored for words but dropping a couple of herring at Hiccup's feet. "In about half an hour, I, Hiccup, will become a fully paid-up member of the Hairy Hooligan tribe."

It *was* too good to be true. Fireworm was just flying back to Snotlout with her twentieth fish, her green cat's eyes snapping with triumph, when Toothless called out:

"S-s-sloppy snob."

Fireworm stopped in mid-air. Her head whipped round, her eyes narrowing.

"WHAT did you say?" hissed Fireworm.

"Oh no," said Hiccup. "No, Toothless, no, don't do it. . . ."

"S-s-sloppy snob," jeered Toothless. "Is that the best you can do? It's p-p-pathetic. Hopeless. U-u-useless. You N-N-Nightmares think you're so cruel but you're s-s-sloppy as scallops."

"YOU," hissed Fireworm, her ears dangerously back as she crept forward through the air like a leopard about to spring, "are a little LIAR."

"And Y-Y-YOU," said Toothless calmly, "are a r-r-rabbit-hearted, s-s-seaweed-brained, w-w-winkle-eating SNOB."

Fireworm went for him.

Toothless streaked off, as quick as lightning, and Fireworm's massive jaws snapped together with a sickening crunch on nothing but thin air.

Chaos ensued.

Fireworm completely lost control. She plunged wildly through the air, claws out, biting anything that moved, and letting out great bursts of flame.

Unfortunately, in the process she accidentally scratched Killer, a dragon with a very short temper. Killer then attacked any Hooligan dragon within biting distance.

Soon the dragons were involved in a full-scale, rip-roaring dragonfight, with the boys running around shouting at them to stop and trying to pull them apart without getting killed themselves. The dragons took absolutely no notice whatsoever, however hard the boys yelled — and Thuggory and Snotlout were very red in the face after some pretty impressive yelling.

Gobber the Belch went ballistic on the sidelines. "CANSOMEBODYTELLMEWHATINTHORAND-WODEN'SNAMEISHAPPENING?"

Toothless was in his element in this kind of chaos, dodging Fireworm's angry lunges with ease, nipping in with a lively bite at Alligatiger here and a

DRagonFight ..
between killer and Fireworm

scratch at Brightclaw there, obviously enjoying the
fight enormously.

Even Horrorcow showed a great deal of spirit
for a dragon who was supposedly vegetarian. She
managed to give Fireworm a truly impressive bite on
the bottom as Fireworm and Killer rolled through the
air biting chunks out of one another.

Gobber the Belch entered the fray, grabbing hold of Fireworm's tail. Fireworm gave a howl of outrage, squirmed round, and set Gobber's beard on fire. With one massive hand Gobber swatted out the fire and with the other he clamped Fireworm's jaws together so she could neither bite nor burn. He tucked the furiously enraged animal under one arm, still holding her mouth closed.

"SSSTOPPP!!!!!" screamed Gobber the Belch with a hair-raising, skin-crawling, fang-dropping yell

that reverberated off the cliffs, bounced off the sea, and whose faint echoes could be heard on the Mainland.

The boys stopped their useless screaming. The dragons stopped in mid-air.

There was an awful silence.

Even the watching crowd went quiet.

This had never happened before. All twenty boys

had shown themselves to be completely out of control of their dragons during the Initiation Test.

Technically, this meant that all of them should be thrown out of their Tribes into exile. And exile in this horrid climate could mean death. Food was scarce, the sea was dangerous, and there were certain wild Tribes in the Isles who were rumoured to be cannibals. . . .

Gobber the Belch stood, lost for words, his beard still smoking.

When he eventually spoke, his voice was deep with the horror of the situation.

"I will have to speak with the Elders of the Tribes," was all he said. He dropped Fireworm on the ground. She had come to her senses and now slunk toward Snotlout, her tail between her legs.

The Elders of the Tribes were Mogadon and Stoick, Gobber himself, and a few more of the more fearsome warriors, such as Terrible Tuffnut, the Vicious Twins, and the Hairy Scary Librarian from the Meathead Public Library. The crowd and the boys stood absolutely still as the Elders consulted in the traditional Elder Huddle, which looked a bit like a rugby scrum.

consulting in the Traditional Elder Huddle

Meanwhile, the storm was getting worse. Huge claps of thunder burst over their heads, the rain poured down, and they couldn't have been much wetter if they had all jumped into the sea.

The Elders consulted for a long time. Mogadon got angry at one point and swung a fist at Tuffnut. A Twin held on to each of his arms until he calmed down again. Eventually Stoick came out of the Huddle and stood before the boys, who were hanging their heads in shame, their dragons at their feet.

If Hiccup had been able to look at his father, he would have seen that Stoick was not his normal, merry, violent self. He looked very solemn indeed.

"Novices of the Tribes," he bellowed grimly, "this

is a very bad day for all of you. You have FAILED the Final Test of the Initiation Program. By the fierce Law of the Inner Isles this means that you should be cast out from the Tribes into exile FOREVER. I do not want to do this, not only because my own son is among you, but also because it will mean that a whole generation of warriors is lost from the Tribes. But we cannot ignore our Law. Only the strong can belong, in case the blood of the Tribes should be weakened. Only Heroes can be Hooligans and Meatheads."

Stoick jabbed a fat finger at the heavens. "Furthermore," he carried on, "the god Thor is really very angry. This is not the moment to weaken our Laws."

Thor let out a great crash of thunder as if to underline this point.

"Under normal circumstances," said Stoick, "the ceremony of exile would start now. But going to sea in weather like this would mean certain death for all concerned. As an act of mercy, I will allow you one more night of shelter under my roof, and first thing tomorrow morning you will be set ashore on the Mainland to fend for yourselves. From this moment forth, you are all banished and may not talk to any other member of your Tribe."

The thunder crashed all around the boys as they stood, heads bowed, in the rain.

"Pity me, for this is saddest thing I have ever had to do, to banish my own son," said Stoick sadly.

The crowd murmured sympathetically, applauding the nobility of their Leader.

"A Chief cannot live like other people," said Stoick, looking almost pleadingly at Hiccup. "He has to decide what is for the good of the Tribe."

Suddenly Hiccup was very angry.

"Well, don't expect ME to pity you!" said Hiccup. "What kind of father thinks his stupid Laws are more important than his own son? And what kind of stupid Tribe is this anyway, that it can't just have ordinary people in it?"

Stoick stood looking down at his son in surprise and shock for a moment. Then he turned round and trudged off. The Tribes were already running off the beach and scrambling up the hillsides toward the shelter of the Village, lightning coming down all around them.

"I'm going to kill you," hissed Snotlout at Hiccup, Fireworm snarling menacingly from his shoulder. "First thing after we're banished, I'm going to kill you," and he ran off after the others.

"I've lost my t-t-tooth," Toothless complained whinily. "C-c-came out when I bit that F-f-fireworm dragon."

Hiccup took no notice. He looked up at the heavens, beside himself with fury as the wind scooped up seawater in handfuls and flung it straight into his face.

"JUST ONCE," yelled Hiccup. "Why couldn't you let me be a Hero JUST ONCE? I didn't want anything amazing, just to pass this STUPID TEST so I could become a proper Viking like everybody else."

Thor's thunder boomed and crackled above him blackly.

"OKAY, THEN," screamed Hiccup, "HIT ME with your stupid lightning. Just do *something* to show you're thinking about me AT ALL."

But there were to be no bolts of lightning for Hiccup. Thor clearly didn't think he was important enough for an answer. The storm moved on out to sea.

11. THOR IS ANGRY

The storm raged through the whole of that night. Hiccup lay unable to sleep as the wind hurled about the walls like fifty dragons trying to get in.

"Let us in, let us in," shrieked the wind. "We're very, very hungry."

Out in the blackness and way out to sea the storm was so wild and the waves so gigantic that they disturbed the sleep of a couple of very ancient Sea Dragons indeed.

The first Dragon was averagely enormous, about the size of a large-ish cliff.

The second Dragon was gobsmackingly vast.

He was that Monster mentioned earlier in this story, the great Beast who had been sleeping off his

Roman picnic for the past six centuries or so, the one who had recently been drifting into a lighter sleep.

The great storm lifted both Dragons gently from the seabed like a couple of sleeping babies, and washed them on the swell of one indescribably enormous wave onto the Long Beach, outside Hiccup's village.

And there they stayed, sleeping peacefully, while the wind shrieked horribly all around them like wild Viking ghosts having a loud party in Valhalla, until the storm blew itself out and the sun came up on a beach full of Dragon and very little else.

♥ ♥ ♥

The first Dragon was enough to give you nightmares.

The second Dragon was enough to give your nightmares nightmares.

Imagine an animal about twenty times as large as a Tyrannosaurus Rex. More like a mountain than a living creature — a great, glistening, evil mountain. He was so encrusted with barnacles he looked like he was wearing a kind of jeweled armor but, where the little crustaceans and the coral couldn't get a grip, in the joints and crannies of him, you could see his true color. A glorious, dark green, it was the color of the ocean itself.

He was awake now, and he had coughed up the last thing he had eaten, the Standard of the Eighth Legion, with its pathetic ribbons still flying bravely. He was using it as a toothpick and the eagle was proving very useful for teasing out those irritating little pieces of flesh that get stuck between your twenty-foot back teeth.

♥ ♥ ♥

The first person to discover the Dragons was Badbreath the Gruff, who set out very early to check how his nets had fared in the storm.

He took one look at the beach, rushed to the Chief's house, and woke him up.

"We have a problem," said Badbreath.

"What do you mean, A PROBLEM?" snapped Stoick the Vast.

Stoick had not slept at all. He had lain awake worrying. What kind of father *did* put his precious Laws before the life of his son? But then what kind of son would fail the precious Laws that his father had looked up to and believed in all his life?

By morning Stoick had made the awesome decision that he was going to reverse the solemn pronouncement he had made on the beach, and un-banish Hiccup and the other boys. "It is WEAK of me, WEAK," said Stoick to himself, gloomily. "Squid-face the Terrible would have banished his son in the twinkling of an eye. Loudmouth the Gouty would have positively enjoyed it. What is the *matter* with me? I should be banished myself, and no doubt that is what Mogadon the Meathead is going to suggest."

All in all, Stoick was not in a state to deal with any more problems.

"There are a couple of humungous Dragons on the Long Beach," said Badbreath.

"Tell them to go away," said Stoick.

"*You* tell them," said Badbreath.

Stoick stomped off to the beach. He returned again looking very thoughtful.

"Did you tell them?" asked Badbreath.

"Tell IT," said Stoick. "The larger Dragon has eaten the smaller one. I didn't like to interrupt. I think I shall call a Council of War."

♥ ♥ ♥

The Hooligans and the Meatheads woke that morning to the terrible sound of the Big Drums summoning them to a Council of War, only used in times of dreadful crisis.

Hiccup awoke with a start. He had hardly slept at all. Toothless, who had crept into bed with Hiccup the night before, was nowhere to be seen and the bed was stone cold, so he had obviously been gone for some time.

Hiccup dragged his clothes on hurriedly. They had dried overnight, and were so stiff with salt that it was like putting on a shirt and leggings made out of wood. He wasn't sure what he was meant to do, as this was the morning he was supposed to go into exile. He followed everybody else to the Great Hall. The Meatheads had spent the night there anyway, because it had not been the weather for camping.

On the way he bumped into Fishlegs. He looked as if he had slept as badly as Hiccup. His glasses were on crooked.

"What's happening?" asked Hiccup. Fishlegs shrugged his shoulders.

"Where's Horrorcow?" asked Hiccup. Fishlegs shrugged his shoulders again.

Hiccup looked around at the crowd pushing its way toward the Great Hall and noticed that there was not a domestic dragon to be seen. Normally they were never far from their Masters' heels and shoulders, yapping and snarling and sneering at each other. There was something faintly sinister about their disappearance. . . .

Nobody else had noticed. There was a tremendous babble of excitement, and such a crush of enormous Vikings that not everybody could get in to the Great Hall, and there was a big jumble of barbarians shouting and shoving outside.

Stoick called for silence.

"I have called you here today," boomed Stoick, "because we have a problem on our hands. A rather large Dragon is sitting on the Long Beach."

The crowd was deeply unimpressed. They were hoping for a more important crisis.

Mogadon voiced the general disapproval.

"The Big Drums are only used in times of ghastly deadly peril," said Mogadon in amazement. "You have summoned us here at a horribly early hour" (Mogadon had not slept well, on the stone floor of the Great Hall with only his helmet for a pillow), "just because of a

DRAGON? I do hope you are not losing your grip, Stoick," he sneered, hoping that he was.

"This is no ordinary Dragon," said Stoick. "This Dragon is HUGE. Enormous. Gobsmackingly vast. I've never seen anything like it. This is more of a mountain than a Dragon."

Not having *seen* the Dragon-mountain, the Vikings remained unimpressed. They were used to bossing dragons about.

"The Dragon," said Stoick, "must of course be moved. But it is a very big Dragon. What should we do, Old Wrinkly? You're the thinker in the tribe."

"You flatter me, Stoick," said Old Wrinkly, who seemed rather amused by the whole thing. "It's a Sea-dragonus Giganticus Maximus, and a particularly big one, I'd say. Very cruel, very intelligent, ravenous appetite. But my field is Early Icelandic Poetry, not large reptiles. Professor Yobbish is the Viking expert on the subject of dragons. Perhaps you should consult his book on the subject."

"Of course!" said Stoick. "*How to Train Your Dragon,* wasn't it? I do believe that Gobber burgled that very book from the Meathead Public Library. . . ." He gave a naughty look at Mogadon the Meathead.

"This is an outrage!" boomed Mogadon. "That book is Meathead property. . . . I demand its instant return or I shall declare war on the spot."

"Oh, put a sock in it, Mogadon," said Stoick. "With wimpy librarians like yours, what can you expect?"

The Hairy Scary Librarian blushed a delicate pink and shook in his size eighteen shoes.

"Baggybum, hand me the book from the fireplace," yelled Stoick.

Baggybum stretched out one of his great octopus arms and picked the book off the shelf. He lobbed it across the heads of the crowd and Stoick caught it, to much cheering. Morale was high. Stoick bowed to the hordes and handed the book to Gobber.

"GOB-BER, GOB-BER, GOB-BER," yelled the crowd. It was Gobber's moment of triumph. A crisis demands a Hero and he knew he was the man for the job. His chest swelled with self-importance.

"Oh, it was nothing really . . . ," he bellowed modestly, "a bit of Basic Burglary you know . . . Keeps me in practice. . . ."

"Sssssh," hissed the crowd like sea snakes, as Gobber cleared his throat.

"How to Train Your Dragon," announced Gobber solemnly. He paused.

"YELL AT IT."

There was another pause.

"And . . . ?" said Stoick. "Yell at it, and . . . ?"

"That's it," said Gobber. "YELL AT IT."

"There's nothing in there about the Seadragonus Giganticus Maximus in particular?" asked Stoick.

Gobber looked through the book again. "Not as such," said Gobber. "Just the bit about yelling at it, really."

"Hmmm," said Stoick. "It's brief, isn't it? I've never noticed before, but it is brief . . . brief but to the point," he added hastily, "like us Vikings. Thank Thor for our experts. Now," said Stoick, in his most Chief-like manner, "since it is such a large Dragon —"

"Vast," interrupted Old Wrinkly happily. "Gigantic. Stupendously enormous. Five times as big as the Big Blue Whale."

"Yes, thank you, Old Wrinkly," said Stoick. "Since it is, indeed, on the rather large side, we're going to need a rather large yell. I want everybody on the clifftops yelling at the same time."

"What shall we yell?" asked Baggybum.

"Something brief and to the point. GO AWAY," said Stoick.

♦ ♦ ♦

The Tribes of Meathead and Hooligan gathered at the top of the cliffs of the Long Beach and looked down at the impossibly vast Serpent stretched out on the sand, smacking its lips as it devoured the last morsels of its late unfortunate companion. It was so big that it seemed unlikely that it could be alive, until you saw it move like an earthquake or a trick of the eyes.

There are times when size really is *important,* thought Hiccup to himself. *And this is one of them.*

Dragons are vain, cruel, and amoral creatures, as I've said. This is all very well when they are a lot smaller than you are. But when a dragon's bad nature is multiplied into something the size of a hillside, how do you deal with it?

Gobber the Belch stepped forward to lead the yelling, as the most respected Yeller among them all. His chest swelled with pride.

"One . . . two . . . three . . ."

Four hundred Viking voices screamed as one: "GO AWAY!" and added for good measure the Viking War Cry.

The Viking War Cry was designed to chill the blood of Viking enemies at the commencement of battle. It is a horrifying, electrifying shriek that begins by mimicking the furious yell of a swooping predator, which then turns into the victim's scream of pure terror, and ends with a horribly realistic imitation of the death-gurgles as he chokes on his own blood. It is a scary noise at the best of times, but shouted altogether by four hundred barbarians at eight o'clock in the morning it was enough to make the mighty Thor himself drop his hammer and cry like a little baby.

There was an impressive silence.

The mighty Dragon then turned his mighty head in their direction.

There were four hundred gasps as a pair of evil, yellow eyes, as big as six tall men, narrowed down to slits.

The Dragon opened its mouth and let out a sound so loud and so terrifying that four or five passing seagulls dropped down dead with fear on the spot. It was a noise that made the Viking War Cry seem like the faint cry of a newborn baby in comparison. It was a terrible, alien, other-worldly noise that promised DEATH and NO MERCY and EVERYTHING AWFUL.

The DRAGON flicked.
GOBBER The BELCH as if
he were a spit ball...

There was another impressive silence.

With one delicate movement of his talon, the Dragon ripped through Gobber's tunic and trousers from head to toe as if he were peeling fruit. Gobber gave a most un-Heroic shriek of outraged modesty. The Dragon placed the same talon upright in front of Gobber the Belch and flicked him like a spitball, way, way away, over the Vikings' heads and over the walled fortifications of the village.

The Dragon put his vast, cracked old paw to his reptilian lips and blew the Vikings a kiss. The kiss streaked through the sky and scored a direct hit on both Stoick and Mogadon's ships, which had survived the storm and were rocking in the safety of Hooligan Harbour. All fifty of them burst simultaneously into flames.

The Vikings ran away from that cliff as fast as their eight hundred legs could carry them.

♦ ♦ ♦

Gobber the Belch had the luck to land on the roof of his own house. The deep layers of soggy grass broke his fall as he went through them, and he ended up sitting stark-naked in his own chair in front of the fire, dazed but unharmed.

"OK, then," said Stoick to four hundred Vikings suddenly looking scared but wildly overexcited, "so the Yelling doesn't work."

They had reassembled in the center of the village.

"And, as our fleet is out of action, we have no means of escape from the island," Stoick continued. "What we need now," he said, trying to sound as if he was on top of the situation, "is for somebody to go and ask the monster whether he comes in PEACE or in WAR."

"I shall go . . . ," volunteered Gobber, who rejoined them at that moment, still determined to be the Hero of the hour. He was trying to sound noble and dignified, but it is very difficult to be truly dignified with grass in your hair and wearing your cousin

GOBBER THE BELCH trying to look tough while dressed in cousin Agatha's dress..

Agatha's dress — which was the only thing Gobber could find to wear in the house.

"Do you speak Dragonese, Gobber?" asked Stoick in surprise.

"Well, no," Gobber admitted. "Nobody here speaks Dragonese. It's forbidden by order of Stoick the Vast, O Hear His Name and Tremble, Ugh, Ugh. Dragons are inferior creatures who we yell at. Dragons might get above themselves if we talk to them. Dragons are tricksy and must be kept in their place."

"Hiccup can speak to dragons," said Fishlegs very quietly, from the middle of the crowd.

"Sssh, Fishlegs," whispered Hiccup, desperately digging his friend in the ribs.

"Well, you can," said Fishlegs stoutly. "Don't you see? This is your chance to be a Hero. And we're all going to die anyway, so you might as well take it. . . ."

"Hiccup can speak to dragons!" shouted Fishlegs, very loudly indeed.

"Hiccup?" said Gobber the Belch.

"HICCUP?" said Stoick the Vast.

"Yes, Hiccup," said Old Wrinkly. "Small boy, red hair, freckles, you were going to put him into exile this morning." Old Wrinkly looked stern. "In order •

that the blood of the Tribes should not be weakened, remember? Your son, Hiccup."

"I know who Hiccup *is*, thank you, Old Wrinkly," said Stoick the Vast, uncomfortably. "Does anyone know *where* he is? HICCUP! Come forward."

"It looks like you could come in useful after all . . . ," Old Wrinkly murmured to himself.

"Here he is!" yelled Fishlegs, patting Hiccup on the back. Hiccup started to wriggle through the crowd until somebody noticed him and dragged him up, and he was passed over everybody's heads and put down in front of Stoick.

"Hiccup," said Stoick. "Is it true that you can talk to dragons?"

Hiccup nodded.

Stoick gave an awkward cough. "This is an embarrassing situation. I know that we were about to banish you from the Tribe. However, if you do what I ask, I am sure I speak for everybody when I say that you can consider yourself un-banished. We stand in awful peril and nobody else in this room can speak Dragonese. Will you go to this monster and ask him whether he comes in PEACE or in WAR?"

Hiccup said nothing.

Stoick coughed again. "You can talk to me," said Stoick. "I've un-banished you."

"So the exile is off, then, is it, Father?" asked Hiccup. "If I go and kill myself talking to this Beast from Hell, I will be considered Heroic enough to join the Tribe of Hooligans?"

Stoick looked more embarrassed than ever. "Absolutely," he said.

"OK, then," said Hiccup. "I'll do it."

Hiccup looking determined

12. THE GREEN DEATH

It is one thing to approach a primeval nightmare when you are part of a crowd of four hundred people. It is quite another to do so on your own. Hiccup had to force himself to put one foot in front of the other.

Stoick offered to send a guard of his finest soldiers, but Hiccup preferred to go alone. "Less chance of anybody doing anything Heroic and stupid," he said.

Although this is the part of the story that the bards tend to focus on as the bit where Hiccup was particularly Heroic, I do not agree. It is a lot easier to be brave when you know you have no alternative. Hiccup knew in his heart of hearts that the Monster intended to kill them all anyway. So he didn't have a lot to lose.

Nonetheless, he was sweating as he peered over the edge of the cliff. There, below him, was the impossibly large Dragon, filling up the beach. It appeared to be asleep.

But an eerie singing was coming from the direction of its belly. The song went something like this:

Watch me, Great Destroyer,
as I settle down to lunch,
Killer whales are tasty 'cos they've
got a lot of crunch.
Great white sharks are scrumptious,
but here's a little tip:
Those teeny weeny pointy teeth can
give a nasty nip. . . .

How odd, thought Hiccup, *he can sing with his mouth shut.*

Hiccup nearly jumped clear out of his leggings when the Dragon opened both his crocodile eyes and spoke directly to him.

"Why so odd?" said the Dragon, who appeared to be amused. "A dragon with his eyes shut is not necessarily asleep, so it follows that a dragon with his mouth shut is not necessarily singing. All is not what it seems. That noise that you hear is not me at all. THAT, my Hero, is the sound of a singing supper."

"A singing supper?" echoed Hiccup, quickly remembering that you should never, ever, look into the eyes of a large, malevolent Dragon like this one.

He fixed his gaze firmly on
one of the Dragon's talons instead.

This was a mistake, as Hiccup suddenly realized
that the Dragon was holding a herd of pathetically
bleating sheep captive under one massive claw. He
pretended to allow one of them to escape, let the
poor animal practically reach the safety of the rocks,
then picked it up by its wool with a delicate pincer
movement and tossed it way, way up into the air.

This was a trick Hiccup had often done himself,
but with blackberries. Now the Dragon threw back
his great head and the woolly speck fell down into the
terrible jaws, which closed behind it with a mighty
crash. There was a horrible sound of crunching as he
chewed and swallowed the unfortunate sheep.

The Dragon saw Hiccup watching him in
fascinated horror and he brought his ridiculously
enormous head down closer to the boy. Hiccup nearly

passed out as his offensive Dragon breath poured out in a disgusting, yellow-green vapor. It was the stench of DEATH itself — a deep, head-spinning stench of decaying matter; of rotting haddock heads and sweating whale; of long-dead shark and despairing souls. The revolting steam curled its way around the boy in repellent coils and wormed its way up into his nose until he coughed and spluttered.

"Some people say you should de-bone a sheep before you eat it," sneered the Dragon confidentially, "but I think it adds just a nice crunch to what would otherwise be a bit of a soggy meal. . . ."

The Dragon burped. The belch came out as a perfect loop of fire that soared through the air like a smoke ring and landed on the heather surrounding Hiccup, setting it alight, so that for a moment he was standing right in the middle of a circle of bright green flames. The heather was damp, however, and the blaze flared for only a few moments, then extinguished itself.

"Ooops," giggled the Dragon evilly. "Pardon me . . . A little party trick. . . ."

He then placed one gigantic claw against the edge of the cliff that Hiccup was standing on.

"Humans, however," continued the Dragon thoughtfully, "humans really *should* be filleted. The spine in particular can be very tickly as it goes down the throat. . . ."

As the Dragon spoke, he extended his claws, the talons slowly emerging from the thick stumps of his fingers and rising up until they resembled nothing more than gigantic razors, six feet wide and twenty feet long, with points on the end like a surgeon's scalpel.

"Removing the human backbone is a delicate job," hissed the Dragon nastily, "but one that I am particularly good at . . . a small incision at the back of the neck" — he gestured at Hiccup's neck — "a swift stroke downward, then flick it out . . . it's practically painless. For ME. . . ."

The Dragon's eyes lit up with the purest pleasure.

Hiccup was thinking very fast indeed. There is nothing like staring Death in the face for speeding up your thoughts. What did he know about dragons that could work against an Invincible Monster like this one?

He could see the Dragon Motivation page he had written in his mind's eye. GRATITUDE: dragons are *never* grateful. FEAR: clearly hopeless. GREED: not a good idea to appeal to at this particular point in time. VANITY and REVENGE: could be useful but he couldn't quite think how. That left JOKES AND RIDDLING TALK. This Dragon looked a bit exalted for jokes. But from his manner of talking he clearly fancied himself as a bit of a philosopher. Maybe Hiccup could buy himself some time if he engaged him in a riddling conversation. . . .

"I've heard of singing *for* your supper," said Hiccup, "but what is *a* singing supper?"

"A good question," said the Dragon, in surprise. "An EXCELLENT question, in fact." He drew back his claws and Hiccup sighed with relief. "It's a long time since the supper has shown such intelligence. They're generally too bound up with their little lives to bother with the Really Big Questions.

"Now let me think," said the Dragon and, as he thought, he forked a protesting sheep on the end of a talon, then chewed on it reflectively. Hiccup was sorry for the sheep but deeply grateful that it wasn't *him* disappearing down the ravenous reptilian gullet.

"How shall I put it, to a brain *so much* smaller and less clever than mine. . . . The thing is, we are all, in a sense, supper. Walking, talking, breathing suppers, that's what we are. Take you, for instance. YOU are about to be eaten by ME, so that makes *you* supper. That's obvious. But even a murderous carnivore like myself will be a supper for worms one day. We're all snatching precious moments from the peaceful jaws of time," said the Dragon cheerfully.

"That's why it's so important," he continued, "for the supper to sing as beautifully as it can."

He gestured to his stomach, from where the voice could still be heard singing, though more and more faintly.

> *Humans can be bland,*
> > *but if you have some salt to hand,*
> *A little bit of brine,*
> > *will make them taste divi-I-I-ne. . . .*

"That PARTICULAR supper," said the Dragon, "that you hear singing now, was a dragon rather smaller than me, but very full of himself. I ate him about half an hour ago."

"Isn't that cannibalism?" asked Hiccup.

"It's delicious," said the Dragon. "Besides, you can't call an ARTIST like myself a CANNIBAL." He sounded a bit exasperated now. "You are very rude for such a small person. What do you want, Little Supper?"

"I have come," said Hiccup, "to find out whether you come in PEACE or in WAR."

"Oh, peace, I think," said the Dragon. "I *am* going to kill you though," he added.

"*All* of us?" asked Hiccup.

"You first," said the Dragon kindly. "And then everybody else when I've had a little nap and got my appetite back. It takes a little while to wake up completely from a Sleep Coma."

"But it's all so unfair!" said Hiccup. "Why do YOU get to eat everybody, just because you're bigger than everybody else?"

"It's the way of the world," said the Dragon. "Besides, you'll find that you come round to my point of view once you're inside me. That's the marvelous thing about digestion. . . . But where are my manners? Let me introduce myself. I am the Green Death. What is your name, Little Supper?"

"Hiccup Horrendous Haddock the Third," said Hiccup.

And the most extraordinary thing happened.

As Hiccup said his name the Green Death trembled, as if a sudden wind had made him shiver. Neither the Green Death nor Hiccup noticed.

"Hmmm . . . ," said the Green Death. "I'm sure I've heard that name somewhere before. But it's rather a mouthful so I shall just call you Little Supper. Now, Little Supper, before I eat you, tell me your problem."

"My problem?" asked Hiccup.

"That's right," said the Dragon. "Your Why-Can't-I-Be-More-Like-My-Father? problem. Your It's-Hard-to-Be-a-Hero problem. Your Snotlout-Would-Make-a-Better-Chief-Than-Me problem. I have helped the problems of many a Supper. Somehow meeting a Really Big Problem like myself seems to put everything else in proportion."

"Let me get this straight," said Hiccup. "You

know all about my father, and me not being a Hero and everything —"

"I can see things like that," said the Green Death modestly.

"— and you want me to tell you my problems and then you're going to eat me?"

"We're back at the beginning again," sighed the Green Death. "We're *all* going to be eaten SOMETIME. You can win yourself some extra time, though, if you're a smart little crabstick. A few scraps from the burning. . . ."

The Green Death yawned.

"I'm suddenly rather tired," he said. "You ARE a clever little crabstick, you've kept me talking for AGES. . . ." and the Dragon yawned again. "I'm too tired to eat you right now, you'll have to come back in a couple of hours . . . and I'll tell you how to deal with your problem then. I have a feeling I can help you. . . ."

And the terrible monster really *did* fall asleep this time, and snored most heavily. His great claws relaxed and fell open and the remaining sheep, their woolly sides trembling with terror, scrambled over the tops of the terrible talons and bolted up the cliff path.

Hiccup stood watching the Dragon thoughtfully for a second, then he trudged slowly back through the heather toward the village.

Everybody cheered when he walked through the gates. He was carried shoulder high and set down in front of his father.

"Well, son," said Stoick. "Does the beast come in PEACE or in WAR?"

"He says he comes in peace," said Hiccup. There were huge hurrahs and heavy stampings of feet.

Hiccup held up his hand for silence.

"He's still going to kill us, though."

...A-a-a-argh...

13. WHEN YELLING DOESN'T WORK

The Dragon slept on as the Council of War argued about what to do next.

"I am going to write a strongly worded letter to Professor Yobbish," said Stoick the Vast. "This book needs a lot more WORDS to tell you what to do if yelling doesn't work."

Which shows how cross Stoick was — he never wrote a letter if he could help it.

Stoick, in fact, was really rattled, for the first time in his life.

This is what comes of not following the Law, he thought to himself. *If I had banished the boys last night like I should have done, they would not be here to die with the rest of us. I should have put my trust in Thor.*

Mogadon the Meathead had not yet realized the gravity of the situation. He thought it was a question of constructing some sort of megaphone machine to make the Yell sound bigger.

"A gigantic dragon just needs a gigantic Yell," he said.

"We already TRIED that, O Plankton Brain," said Stoick.

"WHO ARE YOU CALLING PLANKTON BRAIN?" demanded Mogadon, and they went whisker to whisker like a couple of furious walruses.

Hiccup sighed and walked out of the village.

He had a feeling the grown-ups weren't going to come up with anything fiendishly clever.

To Hiccup's surprise he was followed not only by Fishlegs but by all the Novices from both the Hooligan AND the Meathead tribes.

They stood around Hiccup in a semicircle.

"So, Hiccup," said Thuggory the Meathead. "What are we going to do now, then?"

"Whaddyamean by asking HICCUP?" demanded Snotlout crossly. "You're not going to ask THE USE-LESS to get us out of this mess, are you? He just single-handedly got us all to fail the Final Initiation Test. We were about to be banished and eaten by cannibals all because of HIM. He can't even control a dragon the size of an earwig!"

"Can YOU talk to dragons then, Snotface?" asked Fishlegs.

"I am pleased to say I cannot," said Snotlout, with dignity.

"Well, shut up, then," said Fishlegs.

Snotlout got hold of Fishlegs by the arm and started twisting.

"Nobody, but NOBODY, tells SNOTFACE SNOTLOUT to shut up," hissed Snotlout.

"*I* do," said Thuggory the Meathead. He grabbed Snotlout by the shirt and lifted him clear off the ground. "YOUR dragon got us failed just as much as HIS. I didn't notice *anybody's* dragon sitting up and begging like a good boy in the middle of that dragon-fight. YOU shut up or I will tear you limb from limb and feed you to the gulls, you winkle-hearted, seaweed-brained, limpet-eating PIG."

Snotlout looked into Thuggory's stern little eyes. Snotlout shut up.

Thuggory dropped him and wiped his hands disdainfully on his tunic. "Anyway," said Thuggory, "MY father was on that stupid Council of Elders too. I'm with Hiccup. What kind of father puts his stupid Laws before the life of his son? And what kind of stupid Test

YOU shut up or I will tear you
limb from limb and feed you to the
gulls, you winkle-hearted, seaweed-brained,
limpet-eating **PIG**.

was that, anyway? If we save all those stupid people from a REAL dragon like this one, maybe they'll let us into their stupid Tribe after all."

WELL, WELL, WELL, thought Hiccup. *This is a turn up for the books. Maybe that Dragon was right and he is going to help me with my It's-Hard-to-Be-a-Hero problem. Before he eats me, of course.*

One solo meeting with the Green Death and here were nineteen young barbarians, most of them much bigger and tougher and rougher than Hiccup, looking at Hiccup expectantly to tell them what to do.

Hiccup stood on tiptoe and tried to look like a Hero.

"OK," said Hiccup. "I need some time to think."

"GIVE THE BOY SOME ROOM HERE!" yelled Thuggory, pushing all the others back.

He swept off a rock for Hiccup to sit on.

"You just do all the thinking you need, boyo," said Thuggory. "This is a situation that needs a lot of thought and I have a feeling you're the only one here who can do it. Anybody who can have a twenty-minute conversation with a winged shark the size of a planet and come out of it alive is a better thinker than I am."

Hiccup found himself warming to Thuggory the
Meathead.

"QUIET!" yelled Thuggory. "HICCUP IS
THINKING."

Hiccup thought.

And thought.

♦ ♦ ♦

After about half an hour, Thuggory said: "Whatever
you're thinking about to get rid of that monster
better work for both of them."

"There's ANOTHER Dragon?" asked Hiccup.

Thuggory nodded.

"I went up to the Highest Point and spotted him
while you were having your chat with the Big Green
One."

"OK," said Hiccup. "That's good news, actually.
Let's check out the new Horror."

The trail up to the Highest Point was littered
with scallop shells and dolphins' bones thrown up by
the gigantic storm. Along the way they even passed the
wreck of one of Stoick's favorite ships, the *Pure Adventure*, lost at sea seven years before, and now perched
crazily on a rock three quarters of the way up the
biggest hill on Berk.

Once you were right at the top it was possible to see most of Berk's coastline and the sea encircling you on all sides. Right at the other end of the island, a Dragon entirely filled up Unlandable Cove and spilled over the sides.

He was resting his vast, wicked chin on the cliff as a pillow. Great plumes of violet smoke were belching out of his snoring nostrils.

He was another Seadragonus Giganticus Maximus, this time a glorious deep purple in color and, if anything, slightly larger than the one at Long Beach.

"The Purple Death, I presume," whispered Hiccup, shakily. "This is just what we need. Are you sure there aren't any more?"

Thuggory laughed, slightly hysterically. "I think it's just the two nightmare killing machines. Two not enough for you?"

♥ ♥ ♥

Back at the Highest Point, Hiccup outlined his Plan of Action.

It was Fiendishly Clever — if a bit desperate.

"We aren't big enough to fight these dragons," said Hiccup, "but they *can* fight EACH OTHER. We have to get them *really* angry at one another. We

Hooligans will concentrate on the Green Death and you Meatheads will deal with the Purple Death.

"The one thing we will need is our own dragons, who seem to have disappeared," said Hiccup, "so we'd better start calling for them."

They started calling for their dragons, as loudly as they dared, and then louder still as there was no response.

The twenty dragons that belonged to the Novices were not, in fact, very far away at all. They had made up after the dragon fight and were now hiding in a piece of boggy bracken about a hundred yards or so away from where the boys were standing on the Highest Point. They were crouching like giant cats in the ferns, wicked eyes gleaming. They were now so exactly the shade of a clump of bracken that they seemed to have melted entirely into the bog. If you had been

Newtsbreath

a rabbit or a deer you would not have noticed them until you felt the talons on your back and the hot fire on your neck.

They had been following the boys for a while.

"So," whispered Fireworm, her tongue flickering menacingly. "What do we do now then? The power is shifting on this island. The Masters will not be Masters for much longer. They are trapped, like lobsters in a pot. We are not. We can fly whenever we want. Do we obey or do we desert?"

Dragons are not the sort of creatures to back a loser.

"Whatever we do," grumbled Brightclaw, "let's do it QUICKLY; my wings are freezing up."

Brightclaw

"We could kill the boys now and take them as an offering to the New Master," suggested Seaslug, with a grunt of greedy pleasure.

"What, that great green Devil on the beach?" said Horrorcow placidly. "I don't like the look of him, myself. He has too big an appetite. We might find ourselves as the next offering."

"We fly, then," said Brightclaw, and the others murmured their agreement.

"S-s-silence," hissed Fireworm. "These islands are perilous," she sneered. "We might fly from one danger straight into the mouth of another. I say we obey, until we are *sure* that they have lost. When that time comes I will give the signal for us to desert."

And so, as if from nowhere, Fireworm and Seaslug, Horrorcow and Killer, Brightclaw and Alligatiger and all the other dragons flew out of their hiding place and came circling slowly up to the Highest Point, landing on each boy's outstretched arm.

Last of all came Toothless, complaining horribly.

"Dragons . . . ," said Hiccup.

And he explained the Fiendishly Clever Plan.

14. THE FIENDISHLY CLEVER PLAN

The dragons protested a bit, but the boys yelled them into line.

All except for Toothless, who absolutely refused to join in.

"Y-y-you must be j-j-joking," sneered the little dragon. "I refuse to go anywhere N-N-NEAR a S-S-Seadragonus Giganticus M-M-Maximus. Those things are d-d-dangerous. I shall stay here and watch you all."

Hiccup coaxed and bribed and threatened in vain.

"You see?" said Snotlout. "The Useless can't even get his *own* dragon to carry out his pathetic plan. And THIS is the person you are banking on to get you out of this mess?"

"Ugh," said Dogsbreath the Duhbrain.

"Oh, SHUDDUP, Snotlout," chorused the rest of the boys.

Hiccup sighed and gave up. "OK then,

Toothless, you just stay here and miss all the fun. Now, I want everybody to go down to the Gull's Nesting Place and collect as many birds' feathers as you can for the feather bombs —"

"Birds' feathers!" scoffed Snotlout. "This wimp thinks you can fight an animal like THAT with birds' feathers! Cold steel is the only language a creature like that will understand."

"Dragons have a tendency to asthma," explained Hiccup. "It's all that fire-breathing they do. The smoke gets in their lungs."

"So you think this monster is going to die from asthma right then and there because of a few FEATHER BOMBS? Why not just feed him fried herring and see whether he drops dead of a heart attack in twenty years or so?" jeered Snotlout.

"No," said Hiccup patiently, "the feather bombs are just to make him very confused so he won't kill anybody on the way. Snotlout, Thuggory, I'm going to need to coach Fireworm and Killer in what they have to say," continued Hiccup.

"I'm not putting *my* dragon at risk in this crazy plan," said Snotlout.

"OH YES, YOU ARE," hissed Thuggory,

through gritted teeth, brandishing a massive fist at Snotlout.

"This guy is such a PAIN, Hiccup, I don't know how you put up with him. Listen, Snotfeatures, by some miracle you have got yourself a reasonable dragon. You GET that dragon to do what Hiccup wants or it will give me much pleasure to PERSONALLY boot you all the way to Porpoise Point and back again."

"OK, then," said Snotlout crossly. "But don't blame me when we all get barbecued because of the Useless's mad idea."

♥ ♥ ♥

Hiccup supervised the making of the feather bombs.

The boys gathered great armfuls of feathers from the Gulls' Nesting Place.

They then burgled every item of material they could find: Goggletoad's nappies, Gobber's pajamas, Mogadon the Meathead's tent, Valhallarama's bra — anything they could get their hands on. The grown-ups were too busy consulting amongst themselves to take any notice.

Snotlout cheered up a bit because he could show off his superior skill at Burglary. He managed to steal Baggybum's knickers right off him as he was standing

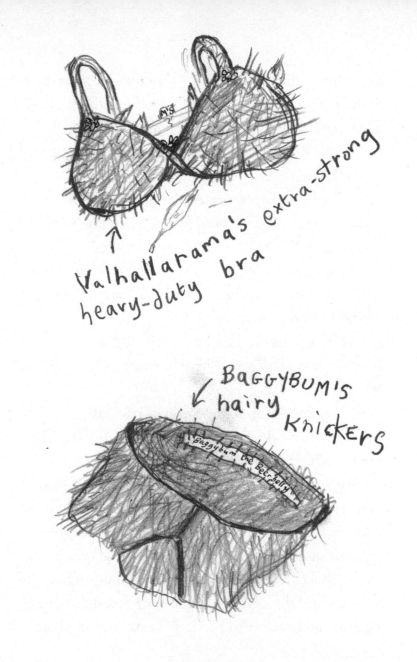

Valhallarama's extra-strong
heavy-duty bra

BAGGYBUM'S
hairy Knickers

Baggybum the Beerbelly

in a Huddle discussing a Plan of Action. Baggybum didn't notice, not even when he reached a hairy hand down to absentmindedly scratch his great bottom — he was too busy talking about Bigger and Better Methods of Yelling.

The boys then wrapped the feathers up in the material, so that they would fly out when the bomb was dropped.

Each team of ten boys was armed with about a hundred of these feather bombs wrapped in a great parcel made out of an old sail.

Hiccup led the Hooligans toward the Long Beach, while Thuggory took the Meatheads to Unlandable Cove.

The thin column of boys were excitedly chattering as they set off behind Hiccup; Wartihog and Clueless dragging the sail at the rear, the dragons circling and diving a couple of feet above their heads. Vikings are practically fearless, having been bred to be soldiers, so even Hiccup and Fishlegs had a surge of excitement at the thought of the battle to come.

But as soon as the monster came into sight again, the boys and the dragons instantly dropped to their tummies and squirmed forward, hearts beating hard.

It was impossible that ANYTHING could be THAT big.

Hiccup led them as near as he dared to the edge of the cliffs surrounding the Long Beach.

They looked down on the terrible creature snoring in front of them. His nostrils alone were as big as six front doors, and the stench reeking out of them made it difficult for the boys to breathe.

Wartihog, who had always had a delicate stomach, threw up disgustingly in the heather.

Hiccup, Fishlegs, and Clueless unwrapped the feather bombs and gave one to each boy. The boys called their dragons, as softly as they could, and each put a feather bomb in their dragon's mouth.

They then stood up on the edge of the cliff with their dragons on their outstretched arms.

This took about the same amount of bravery it might take for you to leap off a mountain at a thousand feet. Even with the monster fast asleep, the natural reaction was to keep hidden in the bracken.

Hiccup tried not to breathe in.

He lifted his arm to give the command to begin.

"Go," whispered Hiccup.

"GO!" yelled back the boys, and ten dragons flew up and circled around the vast sleeping head.

Just as the Green Death inhaled, Hiccup shouted "NOW!" and the dragons let go of the feather bombs.

The Green Death took in a breath that was half air and half feathers. He woke with a gigantic sneeze and, as he shuddered and coughed, Fireworm, who was treading air near his right ear, gave a speech which went something like this, but a lot more irritating:

"Greetings, O Seadragonus Pusillanimus Minimus, from my Father, the Terror of the Seas. He is feeling like feasting on the barbarians and if you get in his way he will feast on YOU. Swim away, little seaslug, and you will be safe — but stay on this island and you will feel the sharpness of his claws and the fierceness of his fire."

Fireworm leads the way in
Operation Sneeze Attack.
Valhallarama's bra makes a particularly
effective double bomb.

The Giant Monster tried to laugh sarcastically and cough at the same time, but this is virtually impossible, and a feather went down the wrong way, making him cough even more.

Then Fireworm bit him on the nose.

It must have felt like a flea bite, but the Monster was outraged.

Through streaming eyes, the Green Death made a swipe at this irritating dragon-flea and missed. One giant claw tore down part of the cliff-face instead.

The nine other dragons had by this time returned to collect more feather bombs from the boys on the cliffs.

"NOW!" yelled Hiccup and, with split-second timing, they let their bombs fly. They hit their target of the Green Death's nostrils and he collapsed with coughing again.

"You cannot win, puny worm," crowed Fireworm. "Wriggle back to the sea where you belong and let my Master have his supper."

Now the Green Death was *really* cross.

He bounded lopsidedly after Fireworm, trying to bat away this irritating little speck of a dragon with his claws.

But the Green Death had the same sort of difficulty in catching Fireworm as you might have if you tried to catch a firefly with your bare hands. Dragons are better than humans at that sort of game but the Green Death kept on missing because his eyes were streaming so much.

"Missed again!" sneered Fireworm, enjoying herself hugely — and she flapped just out of reach of the Green Death's claws. The Green Death made another wild leap toward her as Fireworm flew on around the corner of the cliffs, steering the monster in the direction of Unlandable Cove.

Hiccup and the boys ran after them as fast as they could, but they hadn't a hope of keeping up. Running through heather is not unlike running through knee-deep molasses, and they kept disappearing up to their knees in the bog.

As Fireworm and the Monster got farther and farther ahead in their race along the shore line, it took longer and longer for the other dragons to fly back to the boys and return with more feather bombs.

The military commanders among you will recognize the kind of problems that ensue when the supply line can no longer reach the forces at the front.

Eventually it was taking so long to reload that there came a moment when there were no more feathers tickling the Green Death's nostrils and his eyes stopped streaming and suddenly he could see the maddening Fireworm pinpoint clear. . . .

The Green Death made a lightning reflex swipe at the red dragon and caught her in one gigantic claw.

It was lucky for Fireworm that at that very moment the Purple Death came crashing round the corner and struck the Green Death heavily in the stomach. His grip loosened on Fireworm for a second and she flew off, panting with relief.

The Green Death sat down heavily in the sea and fought for breath.

The Purple Death did much the same.

15. THE BATTLE AT DEATH'S HEAD HEADLAND

While Hiccup and his team had been enraging the Green Death, Thuggory and *his* team had been infuriating the Purple Death.

The two monsters ran smack into one another as they met at the corner of Death's Head Headland.

One of Fireworm's wings was broken in two places from her experience in the Green Death's grip, but she bravely flew back and made her final speech into his ear as he sat gasping for air in the shallows.

"Here he is," shouted Fireworm. "My Master, the Purple Horror, who will tear you limb from limb and spit out your toenails!"

And Fireworm flew away lopsidedly as fast as she could, with one wing trailing behind her.

♦ ♦ ♦

The Green Death was having a bad day.

Ordinarily, a Seadragonus Giganticus Maximus would not dream of attacking another animal of the same breed. They avoid fighting each other because they know they are so heavily armed that the battle risks ending in death for both of them.

However, the Green Death had been attacked and jeered at by minuscule creatures who had inflamed and outraged his vanity. This Creature, who seemed to think he was tougher than the Green Death himself, had struck him heavily in the chest.

The Green Death wasn't thinking too hard.

He leaped at the Purple Death with his talons outstretched, breathing great bursts of fire, which lit up the landscape all around like lightning.

The ground and the sea shook in great earthquakes as the two gigantic monsters lunged crazily at each other, swearing the most unrepeatable oaths in Dragonese.

The Green Death's foot completely destroyed Wrecker's Reef with one blow.

The Purple Death's wings caused great landslides to come tumbling down from the Headland's cliffs.

Now that their job was done, the Viking boys were running away as fast as they could, their eyes popping with terror, in case one of the dragons survived the fight. Every now and then they looked back to see how the battle was going.

With ghastly, eerie cries, the Dragons slashed and bit and tore pieces off one another.

The Sea Dragon is the most well-defended creature that has ever lived on this planet. Its skin is over three feet thick in places, and so encrusted with shells and barnacles that it almost has the effect of armour.

It is also the most well-armed creature that has ever lived on this planet and its razor sharp claws and teeth can rip open its own iron crust as if it were made out of paper. . . .

Now both Dragons had terrible wounds, and their green lifeblood was pouring out of them.

The Green Death gripped the Purple Death around the neck with a deadly Throatchoker Grip.

The Purple Death hugged the Green Death around the chest with a deadly Breathquencher Hug.

Neither would let go — and the grip of a Dragon is a terrible thing. They reminded Hiccup of a picture on one of his father's shields: of two dragons forming a perfect circle as they ate one another, each with a tail in its mouth.

The Dragons thrashed around wildly in the surf, gagging and choking, with their eyes popping, their tails causing such tidal waves that the boys were soaked, even though they were scrambling away from the Headland as fast as they could.

Finally, with some last heaving shudders and grim gurgles, both mighty beasts lay still in the water.

There was silence.

The boys stopped running. They stood gasping for breath, watching the motionless beasts with dread. The boys' dragons, which were flying some way ahead of the boys, also turned, and hung still in the air.

The Terrible Creatures didn't move.

The boys waited two long minutes, as waves lapped gently over the great, motionless bodies.

"They're dead," said Thuggory at last.

The boys started laughing, rather hysterically, now that the terror was over.

"Well done, Hiccup!" Thuggory slapped Hiccup on the back.

But Hiccup was looking worried. He was squinting his eyes and straining to hear something. "I can't hear anything," said Hiccup anxiously.

"You can't hear anything because they're DEAD," said Thuggory joyfully. "Three cheers for Hiccup!"

Halfway through the boys' cheering, Fireworm let out a terrible noise. "DESERT!" she shrieked. "Desert, desert, desert, desert!"

The head of the corpse of the Green Death was slowly lifting up and turning in their direction.

"Uh-oh," said Hiccup.

uh-oh...

16. THE FIENDISHLY CLEVER PLAN GOES WRONG

Hiccup had been listening for the Green Death's Death Song, but he wasn't singing it yet.

The Green Death was dying, but he wasn't dead yet.

What he *was* was very, very angry indeed.

Out of his bleeding mouth he hissed weakly, *"Where is he?"*

And then he heaved himself on to his feet, and hissed a little more strongly, "WHERE is he? Where IS the Little Supper? I knew I recognized him, he was my doom, no wonder. The Little Supper has made a Supper of ME, the Green Death himself!"

As the Dragon spoke, he was inching forward very slowly and painfully, his eyes fixed on the cliff top, where he could see little human beings beginning to run inland again.

The Dragon threw back his head and SCREAMED a blood-chilling scream of pure horrid REVENGE, dark and torturous.

"I'LL supper HIM before I go, I will," said the Dragon, and he leaped forward.

"R-U-U-U-N!" shouted Hiccup, but everybody was already running, as fast as they could.

In the distance, Hiccup could see four hundred warriors from the tribes of Hooligan and Meathead coming toward them from the Highest Point. They must have wondered at the boys' absence and come out to find them.

But they won't get here in time, thought Hiccup, *and even if they do, what can they do?*

Just then, the Dragon landed with a crash on the cliff top and suddenly the sun was blotted out.

Twenty boys ran toward the shelter of the ferns.

The Dragon picked up the nearest with one claw and turned him over.

It was Dogsbreath. By the time the Dragon had tossed him aside, muttering "Not you," the other boys had disappeared into the bracken.

The Dragon was sick, but he laughed weakly. "You're not safe there, oh no, for though I can't see you to kill you, I *can* use my . . . FIRE!"

The bracken caught fire with the Dragon's first breath and the boys ran out of it as fast as they could.

Hiccup stayed in a little longer because he knew the Dragon was waiting for him.

Finally the heat became unbearable and he took a deep breath, closed his eyes, and ran out into the open.

He had run hardly a hundred yards before two of the Dragon's talons closed around his middle and he was lifted up. Way, way up, so the other boys looked like little specks beneath him.

The Dragon held Hiccup up in front of him.

"We are BOTH Supper now, little Supper," he said, and he tossed Hiccup high, high into the air.

As Hiccup somersaulted for the second time he thought to himself, *Now THIS, this really IS the worst moment of my life.*

Then he was falling.

He looked down. There was the Dragon's mouth, wide open like a great, black, cavernous tunnel.

He was going to fall into it.

17. IN THE MOUTH OF THE DRAGON

Hiccup fell into the Dragon's mouth, and its teeth snapped shut behind him like prison doors.

He was falling through complete darkness, surrounded by a smell so awful it was suffocating.

He jerked to a sudden halt as the back of his shirt caught on something and held.

Hiccup hung there in the darkness, swaying gently. By a thousand-to-one chance his shirt had caught on a spear still stuck in the Dragon's throat since his Roman banquet. Hiccup's foot brushed against the wall of what he presumed was the Dragon's throat. The Dragon's digestive juices stung like acid, and he snatched his foot away.

Above him, Hiccup could hear the Dragon's great tongue sloshing and lunging about his mouth, trying to find Hiccup so he could crunch him to death. . . . He hadn't intended to swallow him whole.

A disgusting river of green goo dripped down the puffy red insides of the Dragon's throat. Just across

Hiccup hanging next to the fire holes

from where Hiccup was hanging, greeny-yellow steam was puffing out of two small holes in the slimy wall. Every now and then a small explosion sent little flickers of flame shooting out of the holes.

How interesting, thought Hiccup, who was strangely calm, because he couldn't quite believe that this was really happening. *Those must be where the fire comes from.*

Viking biologists had wondered for years where the fire that dragons breathed came from. Some said the lungs, others the stomach. Hiccup was the first to discover the fire-holes, which are too small to see with the naked eye in a normal-sized dragon.

Way down below him, Hiccup could hear the distant rumbling of singing from the Dragon's previous meal. A Seadragonus Giganticus obviously takes a long time to digest, thought Hiccup.

It was indeed still going strong:

> *Humans can be bland,*
>> *but if you have some salt to hand,*
> *A little bit of brine,*
>> *will make them taste div-I-I-I-ne. . . .*

The spear was gradually bending over with Hiccup's weight. It was only a matter of time before it broke and he fell to join the breezy optimist in the stomach below. . . .

What was worse, the fumes and the heat and the smell were starting to confuse Hiccup so that he no longer really CARED. The terrible noise of the Dragon's heart beating had entered into Hiccup's

chest and forced his own heart to follow the same
rhythm.

A Dragon has to live, after all, he found himself
thinking. And then he remembered the Dragon's
words to him as he stood on the cliff top: "𝔜𝔬𝔲'𝔩𝔩 𝔣𝔦𝔫𝔡
𝔱𝔥𝔞𝔱 𝔶𝔬𝔲 𝔠𝔬𝔪𝔢 𝔯𝔬𝔲𝔫𝔡 𝔱𝔬 𝔪𝔶 𝔭𝔬𝔦𝔫𝔱 𝔬𝔣 𝔳𝔦𝔢𝔴 𝔬𝔫𝔠𝔢 𝔶𝔬𝔲'𝔯𝔢
𝔦𝔫𝔰𝔦𝔡𝔢 𝔪𝔢. . . ."

Oh no! thought Hiccup. *The Dragon's digestion!
It's already working!*

"I need to live, I need to live," he repeated to
himself, over and over again, trying desperately to
block out the Dragon's thoughts.

There was a horrible creaking noise as the stout
Roman spear began to split in two. . . .

18. THE EXTRAORDINARY BRAVERY OF TOOTHLESS

And that would have been the end of Hiccup, if it had not been for the extraordinary bravery of a certain Toothless Daydream.

Toothless, if you remember, had refused to join in the battle at Death's Head Headland. He was intending to fly off somewhere down the coast a bit and lie low till all was safe again, but he stayed at the Highest Point for a while, terrorizing birds and rabbits.

He must have been having a lovely time doing this, for he did not hear the approach of Stoick and the entire Tribes of Hooligan and Meathead until Stoick grabbed him around the neck.

"WHERE IS MY SON?" asked Stoick.

Toothless shrugged his shoulders rudely.

"WHERE IS MY SON???" bawled Stoick with an awe-inspiring yell so loud that Toothless's ears trembled.

Toothless pointed to Death's Head Headland.

"SHOW ME," said Stoick grimly.

Under Stoick's fierce eye, Toothless reluctantly flapped off toward Death's Head Headland, followed by the two Tribes.

They arrived just in time to see the Terrible Monster throw Hiccup high in the air and catch him in his mouth like a whelk.

So much for the Fiendishly Clever Plan, thought Toothless.

He was about to use the opportunity of Stoick's obvious distraction to sneak off to a place of safety when something stopped him.

Nobody knows what that something was.

It was a moment that changed the whole worldview of the Hooligan Tribe. For centuries we had believed it was impossible for dragons to consider a selfless thought or a generous action. But what Toothless did next is impossible to explain as being in his own best interests at the time.

All his fellow domestic dragons were now flying somewhere over the Inner Ocean. As soon as they heard Fireworm's cry of "**Desert!**" those who were hiding in caves or between crevices or crouched in the ferns rose up in a great swarm and abandoned their former Masters as fast as their wings could carry them.

The wild dragons from Wild Dragon Cliff had left hours before.

But something kept Toothless from flying after them — maybe it was Stoick's heartrendingly powerless cry of "N-N-NOOOOO!!!" that caused him to pause. Or maybe somewhere in that self-centered green dragon heart of his, he really was fond of Hiccup and grateful for the hours that he had spent looking after him, not shouting at him, telling him jokes and giving him the biggest and juiciest lobsters.

"Dragons are S-S-SELFISH," argued Toothless to himself. "Dragons are heartless and have no m-m-mercy. That's what m-m-makes us s-s-survivors."

Nonetheless SOMETHING made him turn right

around and SOMETHING made him fold his wings back and fly like a dragon blur to the Great Monster on the cliff tops. Which *really* was *not* in Toothless's best interests, as I said before.

Toothless flew right up the Monster's left nostril and started flying up and down the inside of his nose, tickling it with his wings.

The Sea Dragon lunged up and down, wrinkling his nose like crazy and bellowing.

"A-A-A-AAAAAAAH . . ."

The Creature stuck his great talon up his nose in a disgusting fashion and tried to winkle out the tickling flea that was irritating him.

Toothless didn't quite get out of the way of the talon in time and it scratched him on the chest. He hardly felt it though, he was so excited, and carried on tickling regardless, dodging the probing dragon claw.

"A-A-A-A-A-A-A-A-A-AAAAAAAAH . . ." bellowed the Sea Dragon.

Meanwhile Hiccup was being thrown this way and that inside the Dragon's throat as it shook its head from side to side. He was trying desperately to hang on to the spear, which was in danger of becoming dislodged any second.

"... CHOOOOOOOOOOOOO!"

The Dragon finally sneezed and Hiccup, the spear, Toothless, and a great deal of perfectly revolting Snot were scattered over the surrounding countryside.

Toothless remembered, as he was shooting through the air, that boys can't fly.

He folded his wings and dived after Hiccup, who was rapidly heading toward the ground.

Toothless grabbed hold of Hiccup by the arm and tried to take his weight. Dragons' talons are extraordinarily strong and he was able to break Hiccup's fall, not entirely, but enough so that when Hiccup crashed into the heather he was traveling reasonably slowly.

Stoick came plunging frantically through the grass.

He picked up his son and faced the Monster, holding his shield over Hiccup's unconscious body.

Toothless hid behind Stoick.

The Green Death had recovered from his sneezing fit. He shuffled forward, bleeding horribly from fatal wounds to his chest and throat. He lowered his terrible head till it was on a level with the cliff top, and his evil, yellow eyes looked straight at Stoick.

"Time to die for *all* of us," purred the Green Death. "You can't save his life now, you know. You are quite, quite helpless. My FIRE will melt that shield like butter. . . ."

The Green Death opened his mouth. He slowly sucked in a breath. Stoick tried to grab on to chunks of heather to hold them fast, but Stoick, Hiccup, and Toothless were being dragged slowly but surely toward the gigantic black tunnel that was the Monster's open jaws.

The Green Death paused for a moment before he blew out again, enjoying their terror.

"This is what h-h-happens if you don't listen to the Dragon Law. . . ." shrieked Toothless to himself in horror as he peered around the side of Stoick's cloak.

The Monster puffed out his cheeks and Stoick and Toothless waited for flames to consume them.

But no fire came out.

The Green Death looked very surprised. He puffed out his cheeks and blew a little harder.

And again, no fire.

He tried once more, and now his head seemed to be turning a strange purplish color with the effort of blowing, and it seemed to be swelling, bigger and bigger, as if he was being pumped up with air from the inside.

The Monster had no idea what was happening. He thrashed around wildly and his eyes bulged larger and larger until with a bang that could be heard for hundreds of miles in every direction . . .

. . . the Green Death blew up, right in front of their eyes.

This may seem like some sort of miracle, or an intervention on the part of the gods. But in fact there is a logical explanation. When Hiccup was hanging in the Sea Dragon's throat, desperately repeating "I need to live, I need to live" to himself, he had taken off his helmet and had plugged the horns as hard as he could into the fireholes.

It was a perfect fit.

So, when the Dragon tried to use his fire, the blockage caused a build-up of pressure that eventually grew so great that the Green Death simply exploded.

Now there were pieces of Dragon flying in all directions. Stoick and Toothless were incredibly lucky not to get hit by anything, standing as close to the explosion as they were.

But a single, burning Dragon Tooth, eight feet long (one of the Monster's smaller ones), exploded straight toward Hiccup. The boy had been dragged out from under the shelter of Stoick's shield by the intake of the Monster's breath, and was now lying on the ground a couple of feet in front of Stoick and Toothless, completely exposed.

Stoick caught the movement of the Tooth out of the corner of his eye and flung himself and his shield forward. Only a Viking could have gotten there in time. Shooting woodcock with a bow and arrow develops very quick reflexes.

So Stoick's shield *did* save Hiccup's life after all. If it had not been there, the Tooth would have impaled Hiccup like a prawn on a stick. As it was, it buried itself deep, deep, deep into the bronze center of the shield, and quivered there, blazing with green-edged Dragon flames.

Stoick lifted the shield, terrified that the Tooth might have pierced through to his son. But Hiccup was unharmed. His eyes were open and he was listening for something. He was listening for a strange sound that seemed to be coming from the flaming tooth itself. It was the sound of wheezy, echoing singing, like the wind blowing through coral caves, and it went something like this:

> *I tell the mighty Big Blue Whale,*
> *his life is over soon,*
> *With one swish of this armoured tail*
> *I put out the sun and moon....*
> *The winds and gales are quivering,*
> *when I begin to roar,*
> *The waves themselves are shivering*
> *and trembling back to shore....*

"Listen," said Hiccup, happily, just before he passed out. "The supper is singing."

19. HICCUP THE USEFUL

The four hundred Vikings that were now gathered on the cliff tops broke into wild cheering for Hiccup and Toothless.

They were a strange, barbaric sight, all covered in disgusting green Dragon Snot and Slime, but beaming and shouting with the wild delight of those that have just been saved from Certain Death.

All around them, the terrible fight that had just taken place devastated the landscape. A choking green-gray smoke was hanging around making it difficult to see, but great chunks of Death's Head Headland appeared to have been torn out by the fight. Avalanches of rock were piled up on the beach. The terrible mountainous corpse of the Purple Death lay in the deeper water. Bits of the Green Death's insides and bones were scattered all over the place, while large sections of the heather and ferns were still in flames.

However, by some extraordinary miracle, nearly all the Vikings and their dragons had survived the dreadful battle.

I say "nearly all" because, when Toothless crept

forward to lick the face of his Master with a flickering,
forked tongue, Stoick noticed a ghastly wound on the
little dragon's chest, which was pouring with bright
green blood. The talon of the Green Death had
pierced the very heart of the supposedly heartless little
dragon.

Toothless followed Stoick's gaze and looked
down for the first time. He let out a squeal of terror
and fainted dead away.

♥ ♥ ♥

Two days later, Hiccup woke up, aching all over, and very, very hungry. It was late at night. He was lying in Stoick's own great bed. The room seemed to be crowded with a great deal of people. Stoick was there, and Valhallarama, and Old Wrinkly, and Fishlegs and most of the Elders of the Tribe.

There were dragons there too: Newtsbreath and Hookfang snapping and biting around Stoick's legs, and Horrorcow perched on the end of Hiccup's bed. (The dragons had flown back as soon as they heard the explosion and realized the Masters of Berk were Masters once more. Being dragons, they had given no explanation for their disappearance, but they did have the grace to look a little sheepish.)

"He's alive!" shouted out Stoick in triumph, and everybody began to cheer. Valhallarama gave Hiccup a rousing punch on the shoulder, which is the Viking mother's equivalent of a really big hug.

"We're all here," said Valhallarama, "willing you to wake up."

Hiccup sat straight up in bed, suddenly very awake indeed. "But you're *not* all here," he said. "Where's Toothless?"

Everybody looked shifty, and nobody would look at Hiccup. Stoick cleared his throat awkwardly.

"I'm sorry, son," said Stoick. "But he didn't make it. He died just a few hours ago. The rest of the Tribe are giving him a Hero's Funeral at this very moment. It's a great honor," Stoick continued hurriedly. "He'll be the first dragon ever to be given a proper Viking burial —"

"How did you know he was dead?" Hiccup demanded.

Stoick looked surprised. "Well, you know, the usual: no pulse, no breath, stone cold to the touch. He was quite clearly dead, I'm afraid."

"Oh, HONESTLY, Father," said Hiccup, in a frenzy of exasperation, "don't you know ANYTHING about dragons? That could have been a SLEEP COMA, it's a GOOD SIGN, probably means he's healing himself."

"Oh, Thor's whiskers," said Fishlegs. "They started that funeral half an hour ago. . . ."

"We've got to stop them!" yelled Hiccup. "Dragons are only fairly fireproof. They'll burn him alive!"

Hiccup leaped out of bed with amazing energy, under the circumstances. He ran out of the room and out of the house, followed closely by Fishlegs and Horrorcow.

♦ ♦ ♦

Down at Hooligan Harbor, the awesome ceremony of the Viking Military Funeral was nearly coming to an end.

It was an incredible sight, if Hiccup had been in the mood for it.

The sky was crammed with stars. The sea was glass-flat. The entire tribes of Hooligan and Meathead were gathered motionless on the rocks, and every single person was carrying a lighted torch in one hand.

Even Snotlout was there, trying to look solemn, with his helmet off his head out of respect, and his hair neatly brushed.

"Good riddance to the newt with wings," he was whispering slyly to Dogsbreath the Duhbrain, and Dogsbreath snickered.

"Serve him right for breaking the Law," sneered Fireworm to Seaslug, who was picking his nose on Dogsbreath's shoulder.

A replica of a Viking ship had been put out to sea and was drifting swiftly away from the island of Berk along the path of the moon's reflection, past the

weird shapes of Stoick and Mogadon's burned-out
fleet.

Hiccup could just see the small body of Toothless
laid out in the boat. Beside him lay Stoick's shield, the
Dragon's Tooth still stuck in it like a gigantic alien sword.

Gobber the Belch sounded a mournful signal on
his horn. He was now completely recovered after his
unexpected flight.

"P-P-PARP!!!"

Twenty-six of Stoick's finest archers, standing to
attention at the right of the Harbor, lifted their bows
into the air. Every bow was loaded with an arrow in
flame.

"N-N-NOOOO!!!" yelled Hiccup, with the best
yell he had ever yelled.

But it was too late.

The flaming arrows soared gracefully through the air. They landed on the
ship and set it alight.

Some of the crowd on the shore had
turned to look upward, wondering who dared
to disturb this most solemn ritual.

"HICCUP!" shouted Thuggory the Meathead,
joyfully recognizing the figure on the horizon. There

was a murmur of wonder
from the crowd, as they whispered
"Hiccup?" to each other, then shouted and
cheered and called out his name louder and louder.

Snotlout's jaw dropped open. He looked
thoroughly disappointed to see Hiccup very
much alive and well. Snotlout could just about
take Hiccup as a dead Hero, but a *living* Hiccup
the Hero was going to be very much in the way. . . .

Hiccup was watching the burning ship, tears
pouring down his face.

The boat tipped and Stoick's shield and the
Tooth fell into the water. Just as the last piece of the
boat was about to slip beneath the waves, to be con-
sumed by fire and water, the flames reared up about
twenty feet into the sky. And, shooting out of those
flames, wings spread wide like a Phoenix, trailing fire
from his tail like a comet, came . . . Toothless.

He soared high, high, high into the stars, leaving
a path of flame as he flew. He dived down, down,
down toward the sea, and swooped up at the last
minute, to cries of wonder from the spectators.
Hiccup was anxious that he might be in pain, until
Toothless zoomed low enough over his head for

207

Hiccup to hear the little dragon's rooster cry of triumph.

Whatever Toothless's faults may have been, you have to admire his sense of occasion. Common or Garden dragons are not normally known for their spectacular flying skills, but even a Common or Garden dragon on fire is a spectacle in itself.

Toothless burned through the night sky like a live firework, performing screaming fiery somersaults, and flaming loop-the-loops. The crowd, who only a moment before were expecting to mourn the deaths of both Toothless and possibly Hiccup, were now beside themselves, hysterically cheering as Toothless showered them with sparks.

At last the fire got too hot for him and Toothless plunged into the sea to extinguish himself, only to burst out again and fly straight to Hiccup's shoulder. There he acknowledged the wild applause with solemn bows to right and left, slightly spoiling his dignity with the odd "Cock-a-doodle-doo!" of smug self-congratulation.

Stoick signaled to the crowd for silence, but only so he could boom out the following speech at full blast:

"Hooligans and Meatheads! Terrors of the Seas, Sons of Thor and most feared Masters of the Dragon! I feel humbled to present you with the most recent member of the Hooligan Tribe. I give you my son — HICCUP THE USEFUL!"

And the words "Hiccup the Useful" came echoing down from the hills behind and were shouted back again by the cheering crowd, and were picked up and carried on the night breeze, until the whole world seemed to be telling Hiccup that maybe he was going to be Useful after all.

And that, my friends, *that*, is the Hard Way to Become a Hero.

The Isle OF BERC
DARK AGES

DEEr PrOFESSOr YObbiSH,
I am RiTiNG to complane
moST sTroNGLy about yoor book
'How to Trane Yoor DrAGGon'.
Har You ever tried yeLLing
at one OF those sea Monster
Draggons Yoorself?
Come to Berc and I will
show You wat I mean.
Yours nott very truely,

SToick the VAst

Epilogue by the Hero, Hiccup Horrendous Haddock the Third, the Last of the Great Viking Heroes

The story doesn't end there, of course.

The nineteen boys who entered Initiation with me those many years ago were all allowed into the Hooligan and Meathead Tribes as a result of their Heroic Actions in defeating two Seadragonus Giganticus Maximus in one day. The Battle at Death's Head Headland has passed into Viking legend and will be sung about by the bards while there are still bards to sing.

Of course, there are very few bards left nowadays. What is more, nobody has seen a Seadragonus Giganticus Maximus since, and people are already starting to disbelieve that such a creature could have lived. Learned articles have been written, suggesting that something that large simply could not have sustained its own weight. The dragons that would be my evidence have crawled back into the sea where men cannot follow and, what with Heroism being so unfashionable nowadays, nobody is going to believe the mere word of a Hero like myself.

But the thing about dragons — and I am a person who *knows* about dragons — is that it could very well be that they are merely *sleeping* down there in the black, black depths. There could be numberless numbers of them, all frozen in a Sleep Coma, with the unknowing fishes swimming in and out of their tentacles and hiding in their talons and laying eggs in their ears.

There may yet come a time when Heroes are needed once more.

There may yet come a time when the dragons will come back.

When that time comes, men will need to know something about how to train them and how to fight them, and I hope that this book will be more helpful to the Heroes of the Future than a certain book of the same name was to ME all those many years ago.

It is easy to forget that there were such things as these Monsters.

I forget myself sometimes, but then I look up, as I am looking up now, and I see in my mind's eye a shield, strangely changed by a rich encrusting of jewel-like barnacles and cold-water coral, with an eight-foot tooth sticking right out of the middle of it. I reach out and the edge of that tooth is still so bitingly sharp after all these years that just a gentle brush with the fingers might send a rain of blood down on these pages. And I bend my head, not too close, and I am sure I can just hear very, very faintly:

> *Once I set the sea alight*
> > *with a single fiery breath. . . .*
> *Once I was so mighty that I thought*
> > *my name was Death. . . .*
> *Sing out loud until you're eaten,*
> > *song of melancholy bliss,*
> *For the mighty and the middling*
> > *all shall come to THIS. . . .*

The Supper is still singing.

214

How to Train Your Viking

by Toothless the Dragon

translated from Dragonese by
Cressida Cowell

Toothless was the naughty pet dragon of
Hiccup Horrendous Haddock the Third,
the famous Viking Hero, dragon
whisperer, and awesome swordfighter.

But in this story, Toothless tells a
tale from when Hiccup was a boy, and it
looked very unlikely that he would ever
be a Hero at all…

Snotlout

and Fireworm

GOBBER THE BELCH → ← teacher in charge of the Pirate Training Program

DOGSBREATH THE DUHBRAIN
Snotlout's friend + fellow bully

GOBBER THE BELCH

~ CONTENTS ~

Caliban Caves
Isle of BERK
Wild Dragon Cliff
Hooligan Village
Madman's Gully
Black Heart Bay
Highest Point
HUGE HILL
Harbor
Hooligan
The Little Isles
Cowrie Beach
Puffin Point

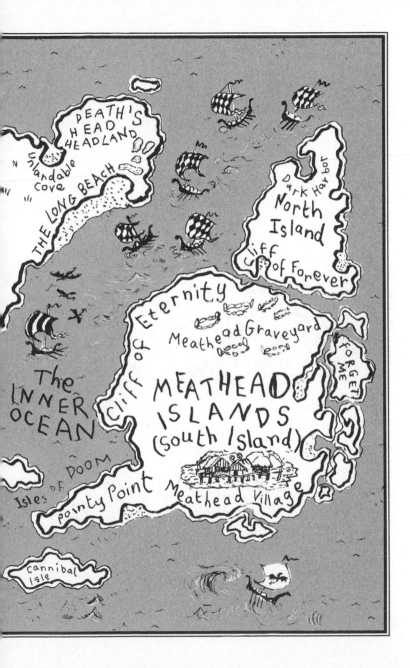

1. A HUNTING COMPETITION

One summer's evening, when I was a dragon so young I had left the egg only five or six years before, ten Viking boys from the Tribe of the Hairy Hooligans stood on a wild and lonesome beach on the wild and lonesome Isle of Berk.

These ten boys were on the Pirate Training Program and standing in front of them was their teacher, an enormous hairy Warrior called Gobber the Belch. Gobber had a helmet with horns that curled like a stag and (like

most Hooligans) a brain the size of a tadpole.

Perched on the shoulder of each boy was a dragon. Some were shielding themselves from the wind with their wings; others were hunched like bad-tempered ravens.

These dragons were hunting dragons and about the size of dogs. Hunting dragons come in many different breeds. There were everyday Common or Garden dragons, with the standard forked tongue and pointy tail, and fat mustard-brown Gronckles with horns like a rhinoceros and teeth like kitchen knives.

There were a few shiny, slippery Slitherhawks with watchful eyes and short tempers, and a friendly, spotted Basic Brown who was chewing the cud as she sat. There was even one enormous blood-red Monstrous Nightmare, rippling with muscles and extra-sharp talons.

Monstrous Nightmares think they are the best breed of all, and they often fancy themselves and put on airs.

I was there too, snuggled down the shirt of my Master, Hiccup Horrendous Haddock the Third, the Heir to the Tribe of the Hairy Hooligans, curled up tightly under his shirt where it was all nice and cozy.

But nobody was quite sure what breed I was.

I looked rather like a Common or Garden with a wart on the end of my nose, but of course I was FAR too special to be such an *ordinary* dragon.

I had been asleep for some time, but it was difficult to doze when Gobber was shouting his mouth off, and his mad yelling had woken me up.

"OKAY, THEN, YOU MISERABLE PIECES OF SHRIMP VOMIT!" yelled Gobber the Belch at the boys. (He always talked like that.) "This is the HUNTING COMPETITION you've been waiting for. In ten minutes' time it will be completely dark. I want you to set

out in your boats, and see how many fish your dragon can catch for you in half an hour…This is a test of how well you have trained your dragon by YELLING at it… for in the dark your dragon will only be able to hear your voice."

These boys, you see, were learning to be Hairy Hooligans, and Hairy Hooligans trained dragons to hunt fish for them and hunt deer for them. Basically, we dragons did all the work, while they stood around YELLING at us.

"Well, Hiccup is going to be even more USELESS at this than he is at everything else," sneered Snotface Snotlout, a tall boy with skull tattoos and a face like a pig. "Hiccup can't YELL for toffee."

This was true.

My Master, Hiccup, wasn't a great Yeller. He was a small, freckly, skinny boy, and he was surprisingly polite for a Viking.

But Hiccup had a very unusual gift. He spoke Dragonese, the language we dragons speak to each other.

Learning to Speak Dragonese

Dragonese can be rather embarrassing to speak because there are lots of odd sounds and accents like whistling, clicking, and strange, low farting noises.

Here are some common phrases:

Pishyou na flicka-flame bum-support.
Please do not set fire to the chair.

Grab-claw di stink-fish or me do di heebi-jeebies.
Just hunt me a haddock, or I'm really going to lose it.

Hoody wobble-di-gats in di bath-juice de mamma?
Who has been sick in my mother's bathwater?

"I don't *need* to yell, do I, Toothless?"
Hiccup whispered to me in Dragonese.
"We're right on top of this hunting business...
you're going to catch more fish than Snotlout
has ever seen in his ENTIRE LIFE, aren't you?"

"W-w-well, yeeees," I said, a bit uncertain-like, but licking his face. I AM a truly MAGNIFICENT hunter, despite being just a *bit* smaller than the other dragons.*

However, today I had this feeling that there might be some reason why this might not work…I just couldn't quite remember what it was…

* Toothless was the smallest hunting dragon anybody had ever seen, then or since.

2. A PROPER VIKING DOESN'T SPEAK TO DRAGONS

"SILENCE!" yelled Gobber the Belch, glowering at us like a bull in a bad mood.

"I do HOPE, Hiccup, that I didn't hear you talking to your animal in that filthy language, *Dragonese*…" He spat out the word like it was a bad whelk. "We YELL at our dragons—YELL at them, Hiccup—and Dragonese is banned by order of your father, Stoick the Vast, O Hear His Name and Tremble, Ugh, Ugh…"

"Yes, sir," muttered Hiccup sadly. He hated anyone mentioning his father. Stoick the Vast was the Chief of the Tribe. He was six foot seven and good at everything, and he expected his son to be the same.

"Now, let me get this absolutely clear," said Fishlegs, Hiccup's best friend. "You want us to go out to sea in our boats when the sun is going to go down in ten minutes'

time and get our dragons to hunt for fish in
TOTAL DARKNESS?"

"You've got it, Fishlegs!" roared Gobber
the Belch happily.

"Ohhhh," moaned Fishlegs. Fishlegs
was even skinnier than Hiccup, and he had
asthma and a squint. "There could be all
sorts of monsters out there in the
darkness…Sea-Dragons…Sharkworms…
Darkbreathers…"

"OH, DON'T BE SO RIDICULOUS,
Fishlegs!" yelled Gobber. "Don't you know
that A VIKING *NEVER*, EVER GETS
FRIGHTENED. Honestly, Fishlegs,
sometimes I wonder whether you and
Hiccup are Vikings *at all*…"

Fishlegs and Hiccup looked
miserable.

"Okay," Gobber continued. "You
have half an hour starting from now, and
the boys who bring back the MOST fish
will be named MOST PROMISING
HUNTERS and will have no homework
for the next three weeks…"

"Yaaaaaay!" cheered the boys.

"...And the boys who bring back the LEAST fish will be named MOST HOPELESS GOATS and will have to give the dragon toilets a thorough cleaning..."

"Yuuucckky..." groaned the boys.

The dragon toilets were in a big pit just to the west of the village, and they were very smelly and disgusting. I never went there myself—*far* too stinky and revolting for ME. I always tried to find a nice, warm, *private* spot to do a poo. In the middle of Stoick the Vast's bed, for example. Or just behind the door of Valhallarama's food cupboard.

As you can imagine, this often got my Master into trouble.

"I will light a bonfire on the beach so that you can find your way home in the dark...*RIGHT!*" boomed Gobber the Belch. "FIND YOURSELVES A PARTNER AND *GET GOING!*"

235

Bathtime

When a dragon has spent the whole day
in a mud wallow and they then want to
curl up in your bed, you have no option.
YOU HAVE TO GIVE THEM A BATH.
Good luck.

Dragon: Me na wash di bum. Me na wash
di face. Me na wash di claws. Me na splishy
oo di splashy ATALL.
I do not want a bath.

You are going to have to be
cunning and use PSYCHOLOGY.

You: Na bathtime ever never ever never.
Me repeeti. Na bathtime EVER NEVER.
On no account are you to get in the bath.

Dragon (whining): Me wanti splishy splashy.
You: Okey dokey, just wun time.
All right, just this once.

You: Hoody drunken di bath juice?
*Who has drunk up the
bathwater?*

Toilet Training

The time has come to toilet train your dragon. You are going to have to be very patient about this. Here are some phrases you might find useful:

You: Toothless, ta COGLET me wantee ta cack-cack in di greenclaw crapspot...
Toothless, you KNOW I want you to poo in the dragon toilets...

Dragon: O yessee, yessee, me coglet...
Yes, yes, I know...

You (pointing at large poo in the middle of Stoick's bed): Erg...questa SA?
So what, then, is THIS?

PAUSE.

Dragon (hopefully): Ummm...un chocklush snik-snak?
Er...a chocolate cookie?

You: Snotta chocklush snik-snak; issa CACK-CACK; issa cack-cack di Toothless NA in di greenclaw crapspot. May oopla hang splosh in di middling di sleepy-slab di pappa.
This isn't a chocolate cookie; it's a POO; it's one of YOUR poos, Toothless, and it ISN'T in the dragon toilets. It's right bang splat in the middle of my father's bed.

3. SNOTLOUT AND DOGSBREATH THE DUHBRAIN

The boys started running toward the six small boats that were drawn up onto the beach.

But before they could get there, Hiccup got tripped up by Snotface Snotlout, and Fishlegs's face was ground into the sand by Dogsbreath the Duhbrain.

"LOSERS!" yelled Snotlout as the bullies ran off, laughing.

Fireworm, Snotlout's dragon, sneered at me before she flapped off: "YOU won't catch any fish *at all* after what happened THIS AFTERNOON..."

Now, this was giving me a BAD FEELING again.

What *had* happened this afternoon? I was still feeling a little confused after my nap and I couldn't quite remember...

By the time Hiccup and Fishlegs reached their boat, *The Hopeful Puffin*, the sun was sinking fast and all the other five boats were way out in the bay with their dragons out fishing like crazy. Fireworm, in particular, we could see diving again and again.

"No problem," said Fishlegs, in between shivers, as he and my Master Hiccup started paddling out to join everybody else. "Toothless can catch up with them. Toothless may be a right pain in the bottom, but Waistline of Woden, he can sure catch fish! In the last two weeks I've never seen anything like it…he is a truly gifted hunting dragon…"

I ignored the bit about being a pain in the bottom (what could Fishlegs be talking about?), and I started swelling up with pride.

"It's t-t-true," I said. "Toothless m-m-marvelous. T-t-toothless brilliant. Toothless the b-b-best…"

Hiccup said nothing. We had reached the fishing grounds by now. Hiccup rolled up his sleeve and put his arm out. I hopped onto it, still crowing.

"Toothless g-g-glorious! Toothless h-h-hunting genius! COCK-A-DOODLE-DOO!" I gloated.

Hiccup interrupted me. "Toothless," he asked seriously. "What DID happen this afternoon?"

I stopped. I looked into my Master's worried blue eyes.

And I suddenly remembered.

4. WHAT HAPPENED THAT AFTERNOON

That afternoon, four hours earlier, I was having a lovely time chasing rabbits, when SUDDENLY from a bush ten meters away there came the sound of slow clapping.

I turned around, and it was Snotlout's dragon, Fireworm, who was clapping.

Fireworm is a bright red Monstrous Nightmare dragon who thinks she is the greatest.

"Oh nice chasing, Toothless," jeered Fireworm, "but why aren't you EATING those rabbits after you catch them?"

My tummy gave a sad little rumble.

"C-c-can't trick ME, Fireworm," I retorted. "Toothless n-n-not eating 'cause he's going to b-b-beat you in tonight's contest...Fireworm's gonna be TOAST tonight..."

"You don't mean to say"—Fireworm laughed—"that you have allowed your Master to BAN you from EATING? I never thought of you as a goody-goody, Toothless..."

I was furious. "T-t-toothless not a goody-goody!" I said.

"Oh, but you are," purred Fireworm. "All the OTHER dragons have been eating...Why, Seaslug and I captured a whole load of nanodragons and had a real FEAST this morning...Ohhh those nanodragons were so TASTY..."

I could feel my mouth beginning to water. Nanodragons are a species of tiny little dragons about the size of insects, and they are a real treat for us larger dragons. I know any humans reading this are a bit squeamish about us dragons eating other dragons...

This is most unfair.

Nanodragons are an entirely different SPECIES from us hunting dragons, as different as a human is from a chicken. And you humans eat chicken, don't you?

There you are then. There is absolutely no difference between you humans eating chicken and us eating scrumptious wriggly little nanodragons.

"Were they the c-c-crunchy kind?" I asked.

"No, they were the ones with the soft centers that melt in the mouth..." replied Fireworm, licking her lips. "We ate so many we had to put some in a barrel in the Old Wrecked Ship to save them for later...But of course that wouldn't interest a GOODY-GOODY like you..."

Fireworm
laughed nastily and
slunk away into
the ferns.

I waited till she
was out of earshot
and then I shouted
out: "S-s-snob!"

And then I
flapped off in the
direction of the Old
Wrecked Ship. And there I
found the barrel that Fireworm was talking
about, and I am ashamed to say, I ate
EVERY SINGLE ONE of those
nanodragons. And they were YUMMY.

I ate so many I couldn't even fly home.
I had to WALK back, groaning, and
it took me several tries to climb up into
my favorite spot in Hiccup's bed. Once
I had managed it I fell immediately into a
deep sleep.

That was where Hiccup had found me,
four hours later, and stuffed me into

his shirt to take me to the Night Hunting
Competition.

THAT was the bad thing that had
happened this afternoon.

5. EVERYTHING GOES WRONG

As soon as I remembered what had
happened, I could feel that nanodragon
feast weighing down my stomach. I felt a
little sick.

I had been TRICKED. From the
look of her, flying around like a buzzard
that had drunk a lot of coffee, Fireworm
hadn't eaten ANYTHING that day at all.
She had TRICKED me.

"What happened this afternoon,
Toothless?" my Master, Hiccup, asked me
again, sternly. I couldn't quite meet his eyes
and shuffled down his arm, shrugging my
shoulders.

"N-n-nothing..." I said.

Hiccup looked relieved.

"Okay, then," he said, getting excited
now. "Let's get going...We've got a bit of work
to do to catch up with Fireworm and Snotlout.
Now, Toothless, just hunt like you've been

hunting for the past two weeks and we should
beat them, no problem. Keep the boat steady
there, Fishlegs..."

Fishlegs swung *The Hopeful Puffin*
around a bit. It was really getting dark now.
You could just see the five other boats
around us in the bay. The other dragons

were climbing high, high into the air and
then diving down into the water to catch
the fish.

"Ready...steady...GO!" said Hiccup,
and he quickly raised the arm that I was
standing on. This was supposed to be the
signal for me to THROW myself into the air.

But nothing happened.

Oh, I *tried* all right, flapping my wings,
struggling to lift off, but that weight in my
stomach just wouldn't let me fly. There I was,
batting those wings up and down, still stuck
like a limpet to Hiccup's arm.

"This isn't the time for messing around,
Toothless!" said Hiccup sharply.

And he repeated, "Ready...steady...GO!"

This time, with a
lot of work, I did
actually make it off
his arm and into the
air. I rose about a
foot or so, flapping
desperately...and

then sank like a stone, hitting the deck of *The Hopeful Puffin* with a nasty thud.

"Toothless!" cried Hiccup, very worried now. "What's the matter? Are you all right? What's wrong with you?"

I rolled around the deck groaning and holding my belly.

Hiccup picked me up. "What's wrong?" he asked again.

I hung my head and covered my eyes with my wings.

In a very muffled voice I told Hiccup what had happened that afternoon.

"S-s-sorry..." I said miserably. I didn't dare look at him.

"Never mind, Toothless," said Hiccup, sighing heavily. "What can you do if people are going to CHEAT?"

At that moment Fireworm came sailing over and perched on the mast.

"Flying problems, little mongrel?" she sneered. "Well, if you will be such a greedy little pig and gorge yourself on nanodragons on a HUNTING DAY..."

"Oh, buzz off, Fireworm, you BIG RED CHEAT..." snapped Hiccup crossly.

"What's happening?" asked Fishlegs, who didn't understand Dragonese, so he wasn't sure what was going on.

Hiccup explained.

"Maybe HORRORCOW could catch us some fish," said Fishlegs, turning desperately to his own dragon. Horrorcow was sitting and singing to herself on one of the benches like a small, peaceful brown-and-white cow.

"Well, you know, boys," she said cozily, "*of course* I'll do my best...but I AM a vegetarian, you know...and hunting isn't my strong point..."

She got slowly to her feet and flapped off, still singing.

"Oh for Thor's sake," cried Fishlegs. "This is TERRIBLE..."

Hiccup tried to cheer him up. "Oh, come on, Fishlegs. It's not that bad..."

"Not that bad?" said Fishlegs. "*Not that bad??* How could it be worse?"

He was so cross he got to his feet and glared furiously at the Heavens. "YOU ANSWER ME, THOR AND WODEN!" he shouted at the sky above, shaking his fist. "It's so UNFAIR! Why do you always let the BAD GUYS win? Why do WE always end up in the dragon toilets? And HOW, oh HOW could this be worse?"

And then the lights went out.

6. IN THE DARK

It was a black moment.

The sun had gone down and we were floating in total darkness. All around us were the cries and shrieks of triumph from the other boys and dragons.

Almost drowned out by this racket, we could just hear the friendly, polite voice of Horrorcow calling, "Cooooee, you guys, where are you? I think I might have found one...Oh I'm *so* sorry, Seaslug, did I bump into you? I *do* apologize..."

Meanwhile, Snotlout's yells were the loudest of all as he bellowed at Fireworm. "*GO* FOR IT, FIREWORM! SLICE THEM, FANG THEM, TEAR THEM TO BITS! THAT'S THE WAY; YOU'RE BEATING EVERYBODY ELSE BY *MILES*; KILL FIREWORM, *KILL*!"

He was almost as loud as Gobber himself, and in that bad, bad moment, you could begin to imagine Snotlout as the next

Chief of the Hairy Hooligans.

And then, in the darkness, you suddenly started to remember all those scary monsters that live in the oceans beneath you.

They were always there, of course, but somehow in the daylight they didn't seem so terrible.

"Sea-Dragons..." moaned Fishlegs in the darkness. "There could be Sea-Dragons underneath us..."

Try to imagine a dragon the size of a MOUNTAIN, a great, evil, glistening mountain with a ravenous appetite and no heart at all, and then you'll have imagined a Sea-Dragon.

"Or even Sharkworms?" groaned Fishlegs.

Sharkworms were dragons that looked remarkably like hammerhead sharks, except that they had legs, of course, being dragons, and therefore they could actually CLIMB ABOARD your ship to get you.

"And what about DARKBREATHERS?"
Fishlegs panicked. "There are loads of
DARKBREATHERS in the Inner Isles...We
could bump into a DARKBREATHER..."

Darkbreathers were bloodsuckers that
swam up from the bottom of the ocean like
vampires and dragged unlucky Vikings down
to the depths where they could do their blood-
sucking in peace and quiet.

But all in all, even thinking about these
horrors didn't seem AS awful as listening to
Snotlout's smug yelling.

"WE'RE GOING TO BE THE MOST
PROMISING HUNTERS THESE
ISLANDS HAVE EVER SEEN! I'M
GOING TO BE THE GREATEST CHIEF
THE HOOLIGANS HAVE EVER HAD!
KILL, FIREWORM, KILL!"

And there I was, lying with a bad
stomachache on the edge of the deck, feeling
so sad that I'd let everybody down, when a
very strange thing happened.

A very strange thing indeed.

The Glowworm

The glowworm is a tiny creature, more like a worm than an actual dragon. These animals are a useful source of light on moonless nights, or in caves. Sometimes the Vikings even put them in lanterns.

~STATISTICS~

COLORS: Gray in daytime, light in nighttime

SIZE: Very small

RADAR: None 0

POISON: None 0

ELECTRICITY: None 0

DEFENSE: None 0

SPEED AND FEAR AND FIGHT FACTOR: None 0

7. THE STRANGE THING THAT HAPPENED

The strange thing that happened was that my stomach began to GLOW.

It gave me a huge shock.

First there was this little flicker inside, and then it got brighter and brighter, just exactly as if there was a light burning deep down in my belly. I was so frightened I ran up and down the ship shrieking horribly because I thought perhaps I was on fire...

I mean, what would YOU do if YOUR tummy suddenly lit up like a bonfire?

Then my Master Hiccup began to laugh. "Toothless," he said, "what KIND of nanodragons were you pigging out on this afternoon? They weren't GLOWWORMS by any chance, were they?"

I stopped running. "T-t-toothless not notice..." I said, but I breathed a huge sigh of relief. Now I came to think of it, they might easily have been glowworms.

Glowworms are a curious type of nanodragon. They look gray and boring in the daytime, but light up like lightbulbs in the dark. I had eaten a whole swarm of the creatures, so now that it was nighttime they were lighting up inside me, turning me into a little dragon candle.

Hiccup and Fishlegs laughed like anything when they realized what was happening. "You must have eaten a LOT of those glowworms," said Hiccup.

"Humph," I said grumpily.

And then Fishlegs stopped laughing.

"Look!" he said, pointing.

I was perched on the rim of the boat, with my stomach sending out light into the darkness. And in the sea on the other side you could just see little dark shapes gathering.

They were FISH, swimming toward the LIGHT my belly was giving out. You may not know this about fish, but they are often drawn toward a light. And in this case, there were not just one or two fish, either. By complete chance, my belly shining like a torch had attracted an entire SHOAL of mackerel.

"*Quick!*" yelled Fishlegs. "Let's get them aboard!"

So that is what they began to do, scooping the fish out of the sea, first with their helmets, and then with an old fishing net that was bundled up under one of the seats of *The Hopeful Puffin*.

You may not believe this, for if it hadn't happened to ME, I am not sure I would even believe it myself. All I can say is, the truth is often stranger than stories.

Now it wasn't so much a question of ME finding the fish, as the FISH finding ME. I had never found hunting so easy in my life. I just hung over the edge of the boat with my stomach shining, and the fish swam up in their many millions and practically threw themselves on deck.

Fishlegs and Hiccup just had to put

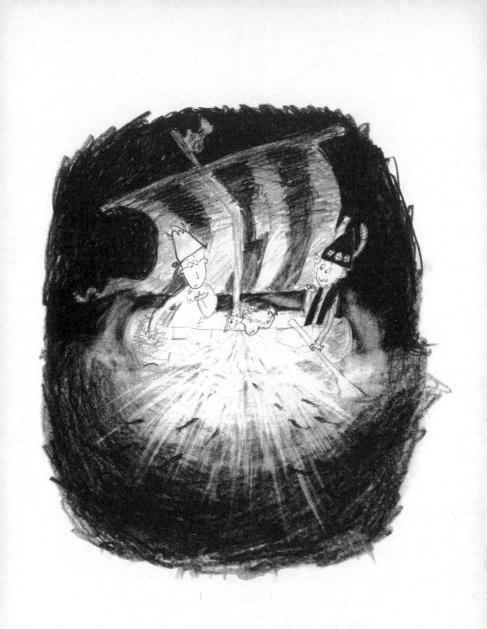

the net in the water, and a minute later it was heaving with a squirming mass of shiny, fat fish. Within a quarter of an hour the deck of *The Hopeful Puffin* was knee-deep in mackerel.

Fishlegs was so delighted he was hopping from one foot to the other in excitement.

"We're going to WIN!" he said. "I just DO NOT believe it…for ONCE in our lives, we are actually going to *win*! We're going to BEAT Snotlout! Fate is on our side and WE'RE going to be the HEROES this time!"

Hiccup was so happy he turned quite white and his freckles all stood out.

"I don't believe it," he said slowly. "It seems too good to be true…"

It *was* too good to be true.

For it wasn't only mackerel that were being attracted by the light on *The Hopeful Puffin*. Something very large and sinister was swimming slowly up from the deep waters beneath.

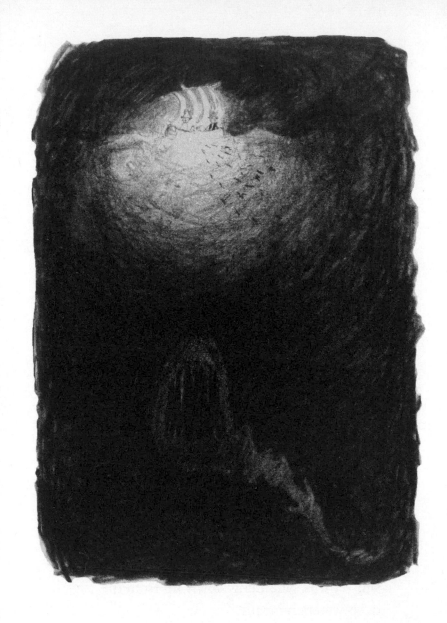

8. THE DARKBREATHER

The Something was a Darkbreather.

A Darkbreather is a dragon that lives way down on the seabed, in a darkness so deep that the blackness enters its soul, if it ever had a soul. They have truly terrible jaws that are bristling with jagged fangs and seem way too large for their snakelike bodies. They lie for hours with their mouths wide open, waiting for the stupid fish to wander in, thinking they are entering an underwater cave.

Darkbreathers cannot survive for long on the surface—too much oxygen poisons them. However, their longing for the light, and their ravenous hunger, draw them upward anyway, and they often snatch Viking fishermen who are leaning out to pull in their nets, and drag them down to the bottom to drink their blood in peace and quiet.

On this occasion it was ME the Darkbreather was after.

One second I was peacefully leaning out, my belly shining like a star, gloating about how I was going to be named the best hunter and thinking of the stupid look on Fireworm's face when she found out. The next, this creature BURST out of the water, its jaws wide open like a great white shark, scattering mackerel in all directions.

I was off the side of that boat and into Hiccup's arms like a streak of lightning. The creature's jaws closed on thin air, and a tiny chunk of *The Hopeful Puffin*'s wooden rims, and the great monster collapsed into the sea again, sending a wave of water over the side that drenched the three of us.

"Aaaaaaaargh!" Hiccup and Fishlegs and I screamed.

Fishlegs made a grab for the sail and started to pull it up the mast.

The Darkbreather

Darkbreathers are dragons that swim up from the bottom of the ocean like vampires and drag unlucky Vikings down to the depths where they can suck their victims' blood in peace and quiet without anyone interrupting them.

~STATISTICS~

COLORS: Dark

ARMED WITH: Enormous mouth and fangs, coils like a snake 9

RADAR: Very good, because eyesight poor 9

POISON: None 0

FEAR AND FIGHT FACTOR: 9

The Darkbreather carried on past us, moving in the same twisting, slithering fashion that a snake moves across the sand. It was already, however, beginning to turn around toward the boat again, slowly, because Darkbreathers don't like to use up too much energy.

"But it will still be able to outrun us…" I heard Hiccup whisper almost to himself.

I could see Hiccup thinking fast. My Master may not be as tough and muscly as the other Vikings, but he's a lot smarter.

"Halt, Darkbreather!" he yelled at the creature in Dragonese.

The Darkbreather stopped for a moment, very surprised that a human could speak the Dragonese language. And then it carried on, easily catching up to us and swimming alongside. I caught my breath. The animal was at least three times as long as *The Hopeful Puffin*, and it was horribly ugly.

When it spoke back to us, it was in a

voice so ghastly and wheezy that it was as if it were coming from the corpse of itself. It was a voice of terrible despair, that came from centuries of living in the dark with no hope, no color, no warmth, no love.

"Give me the star..." it rasped. "I will leave you alone if you give me the star..."

I gave a yelp as I realized the Darkbreather was talking about ME.

"This isn't a star," replied Hiccup, my Master. "This is just a greedy little dragon who has eaten glowworms for lunch...He will no longer be light in the morning."

But the Darkbreather did not hear, or did not want to understand.

"Give me the star..." it repeated with a dreadful sadness.

"No," said Hiccup. "I will NOT give him up."

Hiccup tried to hide me underneath his shirt, but the light inside me still shone out.

"If you want him," said Hiccup, "you will have to swallow the boat."

"All right, then," said the Darkbreather, "I will."

And the monster disappeared underneath the waves.

There was silence for a moment. The wind had really caught the sails of *The Hopeful Puffin* now, and we were skimming along quite fast. Without realizing, however, we had drifted a long way from the beach and Gobber's bonfire was only a pinprick in the distance.

"Where did it go?" asked Fishlegs in terror. "What did you say to it?"

"I told it," said Hiccup, "that if it wanted Toothless, it would have to swallow the boat."

"What did you say *that* for?" shrieked Fishlegs.

"Because I don't think it can do it," answered Hiccup. Curled up tightly against his chest with my eyes closed, I could feel him shivering. "And I wanted the Darkbreather to try *that* rather than put a

hole in the boat, for example. That way we
DEFINITELY die. This way we only
MAYBE die."

"Oh, great," moaned Fishlegs. "Oh,
that's *marvelous*, that is…"

"Anyway, it seems to have gone…" said
Hiccup.

I peered out from under Hiccup's shirt.
Hiccup seemed to be right.

We were getting closer to the beach.
Gobber's bonfire looked brighter and
larger. Ahead of us we could just see the
dark shapes of the boats of the other boys,
coming in to land. All around us the
beams from my belly shone on calm,
shimmering waters.

And then…

About a hundred yards behind us, the
mouth of the beast reared up. It was
extraordinary. For the creature was not SO
much bigger than *The Hopeful Puffin* itself.
But it could open its jaws so incredibly wide
it did not seem physically possible.

Hiccup's mouth fell open also. "That's amazing…" he murmured. "Darkbreathers must have jaws like a snake…"

"Don't go carrying on about jaws NOW!" screamed Fishlegs. "What are we going to DO???"

"There's nothing we CAN do…" said Hiccup.

Now, I want you to imagine the sheer scariness of the situation we found ourselves in. There we were, in our boat in the middle of the ocean, and behind us there was this enormous MOUTH nearly as big as the boat. We were sailing quite fast, but the MOUTH was moving even faster. It was still some way behind us, but it was getting nearer and nearer…

"It's catching up!" screamed Fishlegs.

It *was* catching up.

Nearer and nearer it came, like an appalling moving cavern, until it was so close behind us we could smell the cold, dead-fish stink of its breath on our necks. Fishlegs and Hiccup were both screaming now and desperately paddling to make the poor old *Hopeful Puffin* go faster. Hiccup looked over his shoulder. "I still don't think that mouth is quite big enough to swallow us..."

I looked too. Terrifying as it was, a great yawning cave of death, edged with a twisted mess of razor-sharp teeth, the MOUTH was not quite as high as the mast of *The Hopeful Puffin*.

But then there was a ghastly click, as the jaws stretched just a little bit wider, and then to my utter horror the MOUTH moved under and over us and took us in.

9. IN THE MOUTH OF THE DARKBREATHER

It took us in whole, and the jaws began to shut. I closed my eyes, for I did not want to see the terrible teeth closing in front of me, shutting out the world forever.

But then there was an awful shudder like an earthquake, and another, and I opened my eyes again, and the jaws were still wide open, but the Darkbreather that held us was screaming and jerking and bucking and lashing like a fish out of water. Hiccup and Fishlegs had to hold on tightly so as not to be thrown out of the boat…

…and eventually all was deathly still.

There we were, the boat still jammed absolutely tight in the mouth of the Darkbreather.

But the creature itself was as dead as a stone.

"What happened?" asked Fishlegs shakily.

Hiccup peered upward. "I *think*…" he said slowly, "I think the mast of the boat might have been just too big for it…It may have pierced through the roof of its mouth and into its brain. That's AMAZINGLY lucky, because a Darkbreather's brain is particularly small."

"Oh thank Thor," breathed Fishlegs. "Thank Thor and Woden and Freya and Loki and pretty much everybody, really. We're ALIVE…and tomorrow, I swear, I'm GIVING UP being a Viking; there MUST be a better way to make a living…looking after sheep or playing a musical instrument or making things out of raffia or SOMETHING…Now, let's get back to the beach before I die of the smell of this creature's breath."

This was easier said than done. For *The Hopeful Puffin* was stuck so tightly in the mouth of the Darkbreather that we could not work her free. So Hiccup and Fishlegs had to lean out the front of the boat and the mouth, being very careful not to cut themselves on the Darkbreather's teeth, and paddle this strange combination of boat-inside-creature toward the beach.

It was hard to get going, before Horrorcow came flapping up and lent a hand, or rather a wing, by towing us with a rope made out of that old fishing net. She hadn't found any fish AT ALL, so it was a good thing that we still had the vast pile of mackerel that my belly had caught for us.

10. A VIKING NEVER, EVER GETS FRIGHTENED?

In fact, in the end, it was all worth it.

First, as we just about reached the beach, we bumped into Snotlout and Dogsbreath the Duhbrain, using the last few minutes of the half hour to get Fireworm and Seaslug to catch still more fish.

It was such a pleasure to see the pure terror on their faces as we loomed up behind them. We must have been a ghastly sight, an awful monster with jaws wide open, and me glowing weirdly in the heart of it.

Fireworm screamed, Snotlout turned as white as a piece of paper, and Dogsbreath wobbled with fear like a big red jellyfish.

They were all so frightened that in their yelling and scrambling to get out of the way they managed to overturn their boat,

A-A-R-G-H!

The Sparrowhawk, and they and all their fish tumbled into the sea.

That was good enough in itself. But then, Gobber was waiting with the other boys in front of his bonfire...

As Horrorcow pulled us up onto the beach, Hiccup and Fishlegs still paddling madly, the last little glow in my belly began to flicker on and off.

And when Gobber looked up to see this terrible sight landing on his beach in the darkness, he too turned an awful green color.

Gobber wasn't afraid of monsters, or dragons, or storms, or rival Warriors with axes, or pretty much anything, really, but the one thing he *was* afraid of was GHOSTS. And we did look rather like the ghost of some long-dead creature, with the light in my tummy flickering spookily.

Oh, it did my heart good to see gigantic, bossy Gobber shrinking and shivering and falling to his knees and calling out in a thin little voice that trembled:

"*Whhooooo's theeere??*"

And Hiccup, my Master, decided to teach him a lesson.

"I AM THE GHOST OF THAT CREATURE YOU KILLED TEN YEARS AGO..." Hiccup called out.

The walls of the Darkbreather's mouth made Hiccup's voice echo in the most satisfactory ghostly fashion. "I HAVE COME TO AVENGE MYSELF ON *YOU*, GOBBER THE BELCH, AND THE WHOLE OF THE REST OF THE TRIBE OF THE HAIRY HOOLIGANS...*WELL MAY YOU TREMBLE*, FOR I SHALL MAKE YOU *SUFFER*..."

Behind Gobber, the six tough young thugs, Clueless and Sharpknife and Wartihog and everybody, didn't look so tough anymore. They also fell to their knees.

"Have mercy, Ghost!" begged Gobber, clasping his hands together, and starting to sob. "I didn't mean to kill you...I'm so clumsy; my hand must have slipped...Oh help me, Mummy, *help me*..."

"Just kidding," said Hiccup, hopping out of the boat and over the grim lips of the monster. "It is I, Hiccup Horrendous the Third, who one day will be your CHIEF."

Hiccup strolled over to where Gobber was kneeling and looked his teacher straight in the eye.

"And as you can see, Gobber," said Hiccup sternly, "it is *not true* that A VIKING NEVER, EVER GETS FRIGHTENED. Everybody, and I mean EVERYBODY, is frightened of *something*."

11. THE END

There was an awful silence.

Nobody had EVER dared to speak to Gobber in this way before. I held my breath, and the last dim little blaze of light in my belly went out entirely.

The expression on Gobber's face changed from fear to embarrassment to RAGE.

He staggered to his feet, his brow like thunder, his fists clenched.

And just as he was about to ROAR at Hiccup, something about the royal way the boy was looking at him made Gobber stop.

And instead of being angry, to everyone's astonishment, Gobber's great shoulders heaved, and his mouth twitched, and Gobber threw back his head and laughed.

"HA HA HA HA HA!" bellowed Gobber. "Oh, you had me there, Hiccup; you had me there! Ghost of something I'd killed, indeed!"

And everybody else began to laugh too.

In between gusts of laughter, Gobber went over to *The Hopeful Puffin*, still caught in the jaws of the dead Darkbreather. He admired the great heap of fish on the deck.

"It looks like Hiccup and Fishlegs are the winners of the Hunting Competition!" boomed Gobber the Belch. "THREE CHEERS FOR HICCUP AND FISHLEGS!"

The boys were just in the middle of cheering for Hiccup when Snotlout and Dogsbreath staggered out of the sea, having swum to shore.

"You're *late*!" glowered Gobber. "And where is your boat and your fish?"

"The boat turned over…" muttered Snotlout.

"THE BOAT TURNED OVER?" boomed Gobber. "And you call yourselves *Vikings*? It looks like we've found the

LOSERS of our Hunting Competition...
SNOTLOUT AND DOGSBREATH
THE DUHBRAIN WILL BE MUCKING
OUT THE DRAGON TOILETS FOR
THE NEXT THREE WEEKS!"

Snotlout groaned and Fireworm and Seaslug stuck their tails between their legs and whimpered.

Dogsbreath nearly cried.

It was the perfect end to a day that had turned out fairly perfect after all.

The boys began to rush about getting things ready for a midnight barbecue of all those fish we'd caught. All together, with Gobber's help, they managed to release *The Hopeful Puffin* from the jaws of the Darkbreather. Her mast was slightly bent, but then it had always been a bit crooked anyway.

I had finally digested my meal of glowworms, and so at last I was hungry again, and could do some victory somersaults in the air, and even more importantly, look forward to a nice big mackerel supper.

And it was only I who heard Gobber mutter to himself during the cheering, "Hiccup was right...*EVERYBODY* is frightened of SOMETHING...Perhaps that boy will be Chief of this Tribe one day after all..."

EPILOGUE

Gobber's newfound respect for Hiccup did not last.

A couple of days later, when Hiccup dropped the ball for the seventh time in a bashyball game, Gobber started shouting at him again: "FOR THOR'S SAKE, HICCUP, YOU'RE PLAYING LIKE A FIVE-YEAR-OLD! HONESTLY, MY *GRANNY* COULD DO BETTER THAN THIS AND SHE'S NINETY-SEVEN AND ONLY HAS ONE LEG..." and so on.

And within two weeks, as far as Gobber was concerned, it was as if the hunting-at-night competition had never happened. But *I* never forgot it. How could I forget that glorious time long, long ago in my childhood, when Snotlout and Dogsbreath the Duhbrain had to muck out the dragon toilets for THREE WHOLE WEEKS?

I visited them *every single day*.

Wasn't that kind of me?

And even now that I am an old, old dragon I still sometimes dream that I am shining like a star again, and through the deep waters of my sleep the great despairing mouth of the Darkbreather comes swimming up to swallow me...and Hiccup says again the quiet words: "...I will NOT give him up..."

And he never has.

The Day of the Dreader

by CRESSIDA COWELL

HiCCuP
and his
dragon, Toothless

ABOUT HICCUP

Hiccup Horrendous Haddock the Third was
an awesome swordfighter, a dragon whisperer,
and the greatest Viking Hero that ever lived.
But Hiccup's memoirs look back to when
he was a very ordinary boy, and finding
it hard to be a Hero.

HICCUP
(the Hero
of this story)

TOOTHLESS
(Hiccup's
hunting
dragon)

SNOTLOUT
(Hiccup's
cousin)

FIREWORM
(really mean hunting
dragon belonging to
SNOTLOUT)

THE DREADER
(terrifying Sea-Dragon
keeping everyone
hostage on Berk)

Gobber
the
Belch.
(Warrior in charge of the
Pirate Training Program)

Fishlegs
(Hiccup's best
friend)

STOICK
the
VAST
(Hiccup's father
who is the Chief)

MUM

~ CONTENTS ~

Isle of BERK
Caliban Caves
Wild Dragon Cliff
Hooligan Village
Madman's Gully
Black Heart Bay
Highest Point
HUGE HILL
Harbor
Hooligan
The Little Isles
Cowrie Beach
Puffin Point

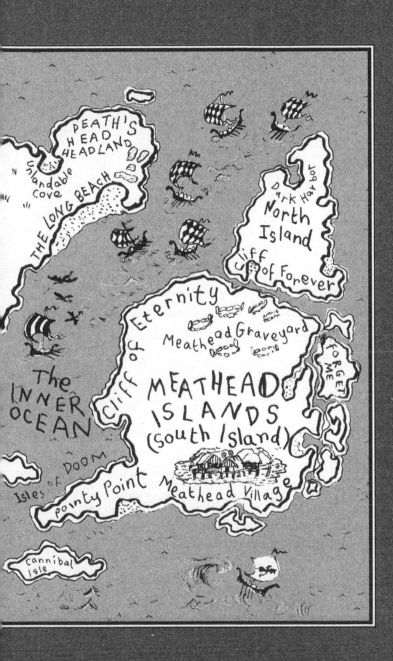

absolutely, completely and TOTALLY

The True Story of the Day of the Dreader

Stories do not always tell the truth. Except for this one. Many stories have been told of what happened on THE DAY OF TH

PROLOGUE

Stories do not always tell the truth…
Except for this one.

Many stories have been told about what
happened on **THE DAY OF THE
DREADER**. Many sagas have been sung
by the bards at the fireside. But I have to
warn you, dear reader or listener, stories do
not always tell the truth. The bard gets
carried away. Legends get added to and
exaggerated, and so gradually, gradually…
the truth gets lost along the way.

Here, for the very first time, I shall tell
you the real story, the truth about what
really happened on that dreadful day…

It *is* the truth, I promise.

One terrible winter, a truly dreadful
Sea-Dragon rose up from the depths of the
ocean like a bad mood from Thor and
swam to the waters surrounding the little
Isle of Berk and took root in the dark mud

there. You could not see him; all that was visible was a long, dark shadow, a deep depression in the water that was so big it was almost as long as the island itself.

The name of that Sea-Dragon was the "Dreader."

The Dreader was no ordinary Sea-Dragon.

Every single dragon in the ocean was frightened of a Dreader.

Sharkworms and Darkbreathers and Doomfangs all scattered like flies at the sight of it. Even a much larger dragon like the mighty Seadragonus Giganticus Maximus, a dragon the size of an underwater mountain, would give a snort of terror when it spotted a Dreader on the horizon, and with one flap of its mighty tail, it would disappear into the depths of the ocean.

For it was said that a Dreader had a power that was truly dreadful indeed.

Legend had it that it sucked out every drop of moisture from its victim's

body, leaving it as thin and desiccated as a piece of paper. Or it merely removed its senses, or its brain or its heart, leaving it mad as a box of frogs, or a lifeless lump of flesh.

The Hooligans were so frightened of the Dreader lurking by their shore, that no boats or hunting dragons could leave the island to hunt fish. They were waiting for the Dreader to go away.

They waited, and waited, and waited.

And as they waited, they ate everything they could find on the little Isle of Berk.

They ate all the fat black mussels that clung to the rocks. They ate all the scallops and oysters and big, juicy clams they could find on the beaches.

But the Dreader would not go away.

And slowly, but surely, the Hooligans and the dragons on the little Isle of Berk began to starve...

Slowly, but
Surely, the
Hooligans began
to STARVE.

Hiccup
Horrendous
HAddock →
the
THiRd.

1. THE CLEVER AND INTELLIGENT PLAN

Six weeks after the Dreader first swam to the Isle of Berk, Hiccup Horrendous Haddock the Third looked up at his father, Stoick the Vast, the Chief of the Hairy Hooligan Tribe.

"I think you're wrong, Father," stammered Hiccup.

The Great Hall on Berk was full to bursting with Hooligan Warriors, slightly less large of belly and chunky of thigh than they had been six weeks before, but still an impressively gigantic and unwashed lot. This mass of muscled, hairy Vikings gave a gasp of horror and turned to gaze at Hiccup, who stood on one leg and turned red to the tips of his ears.

Hiccup was not what you might call a typical Hooligan.

He was thin and clever-looking, with the kind of entirely unmemorable face that does not normally stick out in a crowd. After six weeks of eating very little, he was just skin and bones, and his elbows stuck out of his shirt like sticks.

"Wrong?" bellowed Stoick the Vast. "You think I'm WRONG????"

Stoick, on the other hand, although not as vast as he normally was (owing to the forced diet as a result of the Dreader's presence), still had muscles on his chest that would have made a decent-sized bull weep tears of jealousy.

And when he bellowed, he BELLOWED like a dinosaur declaring war, so these gentle words could have been heard faintly but clearly on the neighboring island.

Hiccup swallowed hard.

"Yes, Father," he repeated defiantly. "I think you're wrong."

Stoick had called an emergency meeting in the Great Hall to present his "Clever and Intelligent Plan for Getting Rid of the Dreader."

Stoick was not the brightest barbarian in the business. In fact, he had just about enough brain cells to keep one gigantic leg moving in front of the other.

So this plan had taken him weeks of sleepless nights, and painful days, with Gobber the Belch holding his sword arm and applying hot towels while he went through the exhausting process of thinking.

And as a result Stoick wasn't too happy about the Clever and Intelligent Plan being criticized.

The Plan was this:

'Stoik the VAST's
'Clevver and
intellijent plan

1. Hole Tribe wakes erly
(to take Creeture by
surprize)

2. Set sail, Bashing axes
on sheelds.
(to conFuse the Creeture)

3. Bash the monster,
untill it dies or swimms.
away.

4. Selebrate with larj
fish Feest and annual bankwet
to bee called from this
moment on : 'THE Day
of the Dredder'

313

"If you provoke the Dreader like this, it might attack out of self-defense," said Hiccup. "I think we should try to talk to it, and ask it what it wants…"

"TALK TO IT?" yelled Stoick. "The speaking of Dragonese is forbidden, as well you know. And legend tells us that the Dreader is one of the most fearsome and supernatural creatures in the Archipelago. Its power is horrific…"

"Well, then," said Hiccup stubbornly, "if we can't talk to it I think we should be patient a little longer, and wait for it to go away."

Stoick the Vast swelled and turned purple with temper. "BE PATIENT?" stormed Stoick the Vast furiously. "I've been eating limpets for the last six weeks! If that's not patience, I don't know what is."

"Yes, but Father—" argued Hiccup.

"SILENCE!" roared Stoick. "The Chief has spoken! Every man, woman, child, and dragon will join in the Clever and

Limpets were yucky!

Intelligent Plan tomorrow! The Dreader must die!"

"ATTACK!" bellowed the Vikings, raising weary arms despite their empty tummies. "The Dreader dies tomorrow!"

Fishlegs, Hiccup's best friend, was the only person in the Hooligan Tribe who was worse at everything Viking-y than Hiccup. Fishlegs had asthma, eczema, and an inconvenient allergy to reptiles.

Now he sighed and said to Hiccup, "You're not going to persuade them, Hiccup. You know what they're like. After a while they just have to go and BASH something, however stupid an idea that is. It's like asking a whole load of overexcited warthogs to be patient."

FISHLEGS
(Hiccup's best friend)

Hiccup sighed too. "I know; I just have a really bad feeling about this Dreader business." Hiccup swallowed. His stomach did a couple of nauseating flip-flops as he thought about some of the things he had found out about the Dreader in the Sagas he had read. "I heard about one Viking ship that had a nasty encounter with a Dreader...and when they came back to the harbor"—Hiccup's voice dropped to a whisper—"every one of them had lost their heads. They were all sitting there, still holding their oars...but not a head on any of them. No wonder all the other dragons are frightened of Dreaders."

Fishlegs sighed and rubbed his neck. "I thought they were just supposed to drive you mad. But they remove your whole head, do they? You see, I'm very fond of my head," said Fishlegs. "Me and my head go way back. Call me old-fashioned, but I'm definitely keen on keeping it right where it is."

Up in the rafters perched the hunting dragons, large as crocodiles, their ribs showing through their thin skin, their eyes watching the cheering Vikings down below. There were Slitherfangs, Gronckles, Monstrous Nightmares—a multitude of dragon species. WHO WILL WIN THE DAY TOMORROW? thought the dragons. WHOEVER IT IS, WE SHALL GET FED AT LAST.

Dragons, you see, are only faithful to their human masters up to a certain point. And the dragons were hungry too.

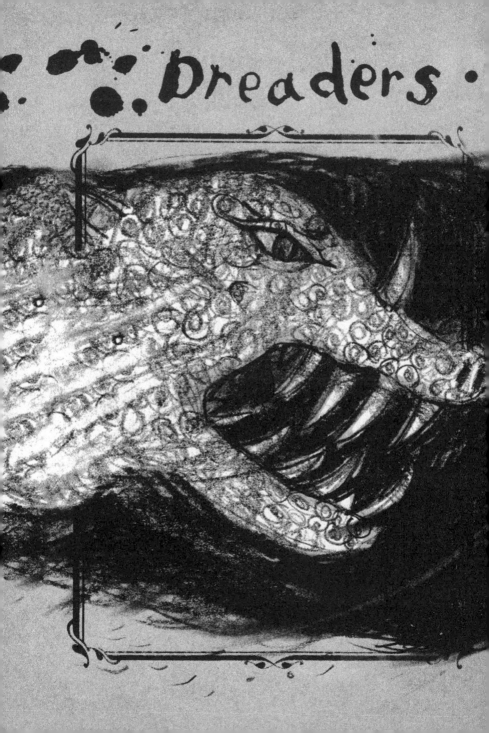

~ STATISTICS ~

FEAR FACTOR: 10
ATTACK: 10
SPEED: 9
SIZE: 10
DISOBEDIENCE: 10

Dreaders are one of the most feared Sea-Dragons in the Archipelago. Great white sharks and killer whales flee like flies at the first hint of a Dreader in their waters. Even the mighty blue whale is frightened of a Dreader. It is said that the Dreader sucks every drop of moisture from its victim's body, leaving it as thin as a piece of paper. Or the Dreader removes the head, or heart, or senses of the victim, leaving it mad as a box of frogs, or a lifeless lump of flesh.

2. WHO'S THE BOSS?

Later that evening, when Hiccup returned home, Stoick, his father, was furious with him.

"How dare you question me in public, Hiccup!" yelled Stoick. "Criticizing my plan, and carrying on about talking to the Dreader, when everyone knows that the speaking of Dragonese is forbidden. Not only is it disloyal to me, it's dangerous. You will be Chief one day and you can't have them thinking you talk to dragons. It's not allowed, and, well, it is a little…weird!"

Hiccup looked miserable. He was always trying to please his father, and somehow he never seemed to.

"Promise me you will not try and talk to this monster!" ordered Stoick. "I don't want you getting too close to it!"

Hiccup mumbled that he promised.

"And another thing!" roared Stoick. "Who do you think did this?"

Stoick held up the chewed remains of a sword belt. *Uh-oh*.

Hiccup's hunting dragon, Toothless, was hiding guiltily under a table.

Toothless was the smallest, cutest, most wriggly Common or Garden hunting dragon that anybody had ever seen, before or since.

He was also the NAUGHTIEST.

"Umm…" muttered Hiccup. "Mice?" he suggested hopefully.

"This was not mice! Those are the gum marks of a fang-free dragon!" yelled Stoick. "YOUR dragon, Hiccup! And I suppose you're going to tell me that those flame-breathing mice have set fire to my priceless spear collection as well?"

Toothless was hiding guiltily under a table.

"That dragon of yours is completely out of control!" screamed Stoick the Vast. "If he's not chewing things, he's burning my underpants. There are scorch marks all over this house. You have to show him who's boss, Hiccup; show him who's boss."

And Stoick the Vast reached under the table with his big, fat arm, and he caught Toothless by the leg and sat him on the table.

"NOW, LISTEN TO ME, JUICELESS OR WHATEVER YOU'RE CALLED," yelled Stoick firmly. "THE NEXT TIME YOU BURN SOMETHING OR CHEW SOMETHING I WILL THROW YOU OUT OF THIS HOUSE FOREVER; DO YOU UNDERSTAND ME?

"You see, Hiccup?" explained Stoick. "It's perfectly simple. I am your boss, so I think up the Clever and Intelligent Plan, and you do as you are told. And you are the boss of Toothless, so you tell him what to do and he does it. Now, I'm going to

need an early night
if I'm going to bash
up that Dreader
tomorrow."

And he gave a gigantic yawn
and stomped off to bed.

Hiccup looked at Toothless
reproachfully.

"You have to stop being so selfish,"
said Hiccup.*

"But T-t-toothless was hungry,"
whined Toothless. "Was Toothless's
tummy's fault. It told Toothless it was so

---

*Hiccup was speaking to his dragon in Dragonese, for
Hiccup was one of the few Vikings, before or since, who
have been able to speak this fascinating language.

empty and Toothless
felt sorry for it..."

Hiccup sighed.

"We're all
hungry, Toothless.
It's so hard
looking after you if
you won't do what you're
told. You *know* the rules;
they're all written up on your star
chart...No chewing my father's stuff..."

"O-o-okay." Toothless nodded so hard
his horns wobbled.

"No pooing inside the house..."

"N-n-n-no, no, no..." agreed
Toothless.

"And absolutely no setting fire to
things..." said Hiccup in his sternest voice.
"You don't want my father throwing you
out, do you?"

"Toothless will be g-g-good!" said
Toothless. "Toothless promises.
Cross Toothless's heart and hope to die:
Toothless will be very, very good."

But I'm afraid I know the truth, and
Toothless had his claws crossed behind
his back.

Learning to Speak Dragonese

Being Polite

TOOTHLESS (to Snotlout and Fireworm):

Yow issa f-f-fishface ickle pinkywriggle wi na scrapers and yow Yellfatter has a sniffer too giganticus, yow may goggla sa fra da starrybit Mars.

You are an ugly little worm
with no claws, and your
Master has a nose so
large you could see it
from the planet Mars.

HICCUP
(to Toothless):
Make sweetispeek, Toothless!
Make sweetispeek!
Be polite, Toothless! Be polite!

TOOTHLESS (to Hiccup):

Quera Toothless make sweetispeek toodi nobrainy greenclaw un Yellfatter meansters?

Why should Toothless be polite to that stupid horrible dragon and his Master?

HICCUP (to Toothless):

Parsk undiless di nobrainy greenclaw and di nobrainy Yellfatter wull scrape us toodi big dreamtime.

Because otherwise they're going to KILL us.

Toothless hiding
under the covers

3. A LITTLE SNACK
FOR TOOTHLESS

The next day, the Hooligans got ready for war against the Dreader, and Toothless refused to go.

"Is not Toothless's fault that big bully Dreader is in the harbor. Nothing to do with Toothless," Toothless sniffed from under the nice warm covers.

"Okay," said Hiccup. "You stay here if you don't want to help, but DON'T LEAVE THIS ROOM, TOOTHLESS. My father is cross enough with you already."

Hiccup looked very silly in his battle kit. He was now so skinny his belt kept slipping down over his hips and tripping him up.

"T-t-toothless do as he's told. Toothless a good dragon," said Toothless. "N-n-no chewing, n-n-no pooing, no burning, Toothless knows..."

But as soon as Toothless heard Hiccup's footsteps padding out the front door, and the sound of those Hooligans thundering down the hillside toward the Harbor, Toothless poked out his snout from under the covers.

"P-p-poor Toothless is hungry," he moaned. "Nobody cares about poor Toothless starving to death. They all so s-s-selfish..." Toothless's fat little belly gave a protesting rumble, as if in agreement. Toothless patted it comfortingly. "D-d-don't you worry, lovely little tummy... Toothless'll feed you...You can rely on Toothless..."

He gave a sudden squeal of excitement. He had just remembered. A couple of months ago, he had buried three eggs just outside the Great Hall. Toothless often hid little snacks like this so that he could enjoy them at a later date, but with all the excitement about the Dreader he had completely forgotten about this particular little treat.

Toothless swooped through the
smoke in the empty hall and out through
the open door. There was a scrabbly patch
of grass and gorse bushes and bracken in
front of the Great Hall, and Toothless flew
over it several times, his sharp little
greengage eyes searching for something.
Eventually he found the right spot and
started digging vigorously with his
front paws.

The ferns shook maniacally for a couple
of minutes, mud spraying upward like a
dirt volcano, until Toothless unearthed
three large eggs, a beautiful lime green in
color, and lightly speckled with pale brown
freckles. Toothless licked his lips with his
forked tongue, mouth watering already.
FOOD.

There was nothing Toothless liked more
than a delicious egg. Boiled eggs, fried
eggs, coddled eggs, you name it: Toothless
liked them any way at all.

But Toothless was particularly fond of a
baked egg, cooked for just long enough

that the yoke was still runny but the white was firm and scrumptious.

Toothless began to roll the eggs toward the open door of the Great Hall, using the end of his snout and his wings. It was quite tricky rolling three of them at once, as they tended to go off in opposite directions, and he had to be very gentle, for fear of cracking them. Once he'd gotten them through the front door it was easier, for the Great Hall had a smooth dirt floor, just right for rolling. Triumphantly, Toothless rolled the eggs over the floor, and one, two, three, *right* into the ashes of the fire smoking on the hearthstone.

Then, cooing with greed, he tenderly scooped the ash over them with his wings, so that they were completely buried in the hot gray dust. (Toothless's skin, like all dragon skin, was fairly fireproof, so he could do this without hurting himself.)

Chirping with satisfaction, and drooling with excitement, Toothless

perched on one leg on top of the meat spit
to wait for them to cook, blinking fondly at
the little mounds in the ash.

one ... two .... three

dragon eggs.

4. IS THERE SUCH A THING AS A HAUNTED EGG?

After about two minutes, something strange happened.

The ash around the eggs turned lime green, and the eggs themselves began to shake, and one of them shook so hard that it wobbled itself right out of the ash and rolled onto the floor again. Squeaking with alarm, Toothless shepherded it back into the ash again, muttering, "N-n-not ready yet! You're not ready!"

But no sooner had he gotten one egg safely back and buried in the ash than another rolled off in a completely different direction. Squealing and baffled, Toothless swooped after one, and then the other, scooping them back into the fire with his wings, like an anxious mother hen with her disobedient chicks. But they kept on rolling out again, and before long Toothless

was out of breath, indignant, and covered
with ash.

Finally, he maneuvered one of the eggs
all the way back from the other side of the
room for the fifth time, and buried it
lovingly next to its fellows, and there was a
brief moment when all three lay still, as
they should be. "Th-th-there," said
Toothless with a grunt of satisfaction—and
all three gave a violent tremble at the same

time, as if they were in
secret communication with
one another, and rocked
fiercely out of the fire bed, bowling around
the room in wild, wandering circles.

Toothless sat down heavily in the fire,
in his bewilderment, putting out the last
remains of the flames with his bottom. He
followed the lunatic progress of the eggs
with his eyes as they looped crazily around
the dust of the Great Hall, gathering speed
as they went.

"W-w-what's going on?" squeaked
Toothless. "Stay h-h-here and do as you're
told!"

Food shouldn't run away like this. It
should stay still, and let itself be cooked,

like any self-respecting sausage or carrot. It
shouldn't be running around the room as if
it had a mind of its own, weaving its way
through the chair legs and generally
showing off.

One of the eggs had come to rest
against a table leg. Crouching down low,
Toothless stalked the egg slowly,
as if it were prey. The egg did
not move. Feeling braver,
Toothless edged a little closer. The
egg remained motionless. Toothless
froze, ready to pounce, whiskers
quivering faintly, every muscle tense. The
egg was egg-ily still.

Toothless sprang…and just at the
last minute the egg wobbled wildly to life,
swerving out of the way and skittering out
of reach, so that poor Toothless's paws
closed on nothing, and the momentum
carried him forward, and he bashed his
nose on the table leg.

"Rrreeeowww…" Toothless let out
a strangled meowing noise like a cat

that has had its tail pulled.

And *"Tee-hee-hee-hee-hee..."* came the sound from the egg, gently vibrating on the spot. Toothless could have sworn it was tittering. Muffled giggling noises came from the two other eggs, on the other sides of the room.

Now poor Toothless was thoroughly terrified. He stuck his tail between his legs and whimpered pathetically.

"H-H-H-HAUNTED eggs!" moaned poor Toothless. Probably inhabited by the ghosts of vengeful suppers that Toothless had burgled over the years, and let's face it, there were loads of those.

It was the only explanation. Just as he was backing away, the spines on his back quivering like porcupine needles, there was a loud CRACK!

...and crooked little lines appeared all over the lime-green surface of the egg.
CRACK! CRACK! CRACK!

A hard little head punched its way through the eggshell (it had to be hard, for the shells of dragon eggs are nearly a centimeter thick). A tiny little dragon, with huge yellow eyes and a black smudge on the end of its nose, blinked back at an astonished Toothless.

And after a gob-smacked minute while Toothless digested this latest surprising development:

"Papa!" squeaked the little smudgy dragon. "Papa! Papa! Papa!"

5. TOOTHLESS IS NOT YOUR PAPA

With every "Papa!" the tiny creature head-butted the shell that was still partly encasing him, until with a final CRACK! the dragon unfolded its wet little wings and the egg fell apart entirely into tiny smashed pieces of green.

The dragon was far smaller than the size of the egg that had encased it, a little larger perhaps than a baby chick or duckling, but not a lot. It was covered all over with lime-green goo, and as it shook out its wings, the startling orange of a scallop coral, it flung a fine rain of gooey stuff over Toothless himself.

"Y-y-yucky," groaned Toothless.

The little dragon grinned. "Papa," it repeated, looking up at him lovingly.

Toothless was horrified. "Me? Toothless not your P-p-papa. Toothless HATES babies..."

The dragon baby ignored this and hopped toward Toothless enthusiastically. "Papa!"

CRACK! CRACK! CRACK!

The other two eggs split apart too, on opposite sides of the room.

"Papa!"

"Papa!"

Two more little dragon babies hopped out of the smashed remains of their shells and hopped unsteadily toward Toothless.

The second one was yellow rather than green and had a remarkably flat head, because it had spent its egg-hood bashing against the walls of the shell. The third was a bit smaller and bright blue and kept on falling over because it had a rather wobbly leg and a permanent case of the hiccups.

One... two... three

little dragons

It tended to
charge ahead in an
uncontrolled fashion as if its legs
had run away with it, before leaning to
the left and landing on its bottom and
saying "Whoops!" in a surprised fashion.
Although why it was surprised I have no
idea because it fell over pretty much every
two minutes, so it shouldn't have been
much of a shock when it did it again.

It also had a terrible cold, so every now
and then it added "Aaatishoo!" to the
"Hic!," "Whoops," and "Ow!"s.

"Papa!" squealed the second one
gruffly.

"It's our Papa! Hic! Whoops...Ow...
ATISHOO!" said the third one.

"Toothless N-N-NOT your Papa," said
Toothless firmly, backing away as the little
creatures rushed toward him in a flurry of
green goo.

"Toothless not like babies...

B-b-babies is yucky and wet, and ever so soppy..."

These babies were certainly all that, but they carried on rushing toward him in a yucky, soppy, gooey mess nonetheless, and he had to take off suddenly so that the little blue one bashed into all the others, and Toothless flapped up to perch on one of the ceiling beams and blinked down at them furiously. They couldn't yet fly, so they couldn't follow him; they just leaped up and down, cheeping and clicking furiously.

Toothless tucked his head under his wing and pretended to go to sleep.

Five minutes later they were still there, cheeping and clicking and bouncing more hysterically than ever. "Papa! Papa! Papa!"

Oh fishhooks.

Toothless would never live it down with the

little GREEN dragon

little YELLOW dragon

little BLUE dragon

other dragons if he kept on being followed about by soppy little dragon babies.

"GO AWAY! Toothless NOT your Papa...Toothless just tried to eat you... Toothless could *still* eat you..." Toothless shouted down from the roof beam.

In fact, Toothless ate pretty much anything, but even *he* drew the line at baby dragons who thought you were their father. However, from Toothless's perch, he had a great view out of one of the high windows.

Through the window, he caught sight of a red dragon flying toward the house, still some distance away.

Fireworm.

Fireworm would take care of the problem. You see, Fireworm was a Monstrous Nightmare and did not suffer from any of Toothless's rare qualms of conscience, and she would gobble up three insufferably cute little dragons in less time than it took a dragon to scratch its own ear. The cuter the better, as far as Fireworm was concerned.

Toothless grinned. She was definitely flying their way, probably hoping that Stoick had left some tidbits over from breakfast. Toothless settled down more comfortably on the roof beam to wait for her to show up. It wouldn't be *his* fault if Fireworm decided to eat them, would it?

The moment that Fireworm set eyes on those babies, they would be doomed...

6. THE TERRIBLE POWER OF THE DREADER

I'm sorry; it doesn't seem a very good moment, but we'll just have to leave those babies in awful peril, about to be eaten up by Fireworm, while we return to catch up with what was happening with Hiccup and the Hooligans.

Because they were in trouble too, you see.

Dreadful, ghastly trouble.

Trouble too nasty to even *think* about, let alone tell.

The Hooligans were aboard their ships, and the ships were already out

in the bay, carrying out Stoick's Clever and
Intelligent Plan.

They were advancing on that great,
grim underwater shadow, banging on their
shields with their axes to shoo away this
terrible beast.

Even the bravest of the Hooligans,
magnificent warriors like that gormless
muscular giant, Gobber the Belch, were
terrified, and white to the lips.

All their senses told them to "Go
back!" To run away from that darkness
under the waves, and not to go nearer.

"Go back! Go back! Go back!"

But hunger had made them
desperate.

So they *forced* their quaking, hairy
arms to row toward the dreadful shadow.

They *made* their poor exhausted limbs bash those axes weakly on those shields and *ordered* their poor shaking feet to drum out a pathetic human warning to the mighty, pitiless horror that was lurking under the water.

It was very, very brave of those Hooligans.

It was also extremely stupid.

Hiccup and Fishlegs were aboard Stoick's ship, *The Fat Penguin*.

Fishlegs was trembling all over, his legs shivering uncontrollably, as if he had caught some feverish plague. He had his eyes closed, in the useless and pathetic hope that if he couldn't *see* what was happening, maybe he wasn't really there.

He tried to bash his axe on his shaking shield, moaning, "Oh, this noise really isn't helping my headache one bit…"

Fishlegs laughed, but the laugh grew out of control and became a bit hysterical. "What's going on, Hiccup? Has the Dreader sucked out anybody's

Oh... this noise isn't helpinG my headache ONE BIT.

heart or removed their head yet?"

"Not yet," replied Hiccup cautiously.
He too was pale as death, heart beating so
quickly he felt sick with the pulse of it.
This was going to be a really unpleasant
way to die...

And then, in front of Hiccup's terrified
eyes, a miracle happened.

"Hang on a second," panted Hiccup in
joyous astonishment. "I don't believe it...
It's turning...It's moving away!"

And so it seemed. The dark shape uncurled its serpentine coils from around the island. It moved away, out into the sea that was Woden's bathtub, and as it moved, the famished Vikings could hardly believe their luck.

Terror turned to hope in an instant.

The hope gave strength to their arms, and they increased their banging on the shields and let out a ragged Hooligan hoorah, as they saw themselves being able to fish for food for the first time in many, many weeks.

"Bring out the nets!" bellowed Stoick the Keen-to-Be-Vast-Again, red with relief.

Thank Thor, thank Thor.

For one horrible moment, he had thought perhaps his plan hadn't been such a good one after all. He shook his sword and patted his poor empty belly.

"You see, Hiccup?" Flushed and beaming with triumph, Stoick turned to his son. "The plan is working, my boy."

He patted Hiccup kindly on the head. "Watch and learn, Hiccup laddie, watch and learn. My Clever and Intelligent Plan is working. Thinking skills, you see. Brain power."

Stoick tapped his hairy head importantly, and then roared to the Viking warriors in relieved joy: "THERE WILL BE FEASTING TONIGHT, BY THE STOMACH JUICES OF THOR, THERE WILL, MY FELLOW HOOLIGANS!"

But WHO would be feasting on WHOM???

Sometimes we rejoice too soon, brothers and sisters.

Sometimes we rejoice too soon, and

we forget we are not safe until we reach the shore, or the end of the story, whichever is nearer.

It seemed that the Hooligans *had* rejoiced too soon, for slowly, slowly the shadow that had been moving away, like a departing underwater battleship, slowly, slowly, came to a halt.

Slowly, slowly, the shadow turned again...

It turned to face the Hooligan fleet.

Stoick was not what you might call a lightning thinker, but even *he* realized that this was not good news. His mouth dropped open. "Uh-oh."

And the Hooligan hurrah died on famished lips, and all around the ships the Hooligans stopped banging on their shields, and the noise came to a confused halt as their poor, weakened arms were frozen in terror.

All except for Fishlegs, who banged away more shakily than ever, squeaking, "Why are they stopping, Hiccup? Why are

CLANG!

CLANG!

CLANG!

they stopping? Actually, don't tell me...I don't want to know."

Hiccup, peering out into the darkness, swallowed hard, though his mouth had no moisture, for it was dry as dust.

"Don't open your eyes yet, Fishlegs," was all he said.

The shadow was moving…

Oh for Thor's sake, it was huge…

It was moving, moving, and the darkened sea swelled up and began to surge toward them like a tidal wave, but it wasn't a tidal wave at all…

It was the Dreader.

7. THE ATTACK OF THE DREADER

There was a dreadful, ghastly silence.

And then the Hooligans lost it.

Relief turned back to terror again in an instant.

They forgot their empty bellies, and their pride, and the Clever and Intelligent Plan.

All they saw was the shadow, that hole in the water that they filled up with their worst, their darkest, their most terrible fears…

And then "MAKE FOR THE SHORE!" bellowed Stoick the Vast, and they hauled on the sail like wild things, trying to change direction and go back to the harbor, for the wind was carrying them straight into the path of the charging beast.

Only Fishlegs banged away madly at his shield, eyes tightly shut, shouting,

"Don't tell me what's happening! Don't tell me what's happening!"

But Hiccup couldn't have told him what was happening anyway.

Hiccup, you see, had forgotten the promise that he had made his father.

He was already leaning over the side of the boat, shouting at the Dreader in the water, the shadow that was gaining on them…

Just to make things even worse, the wind had died.

The sail was flapping and sagging uselessly as the Dreader stormed toward them.

It was as if they were in one of those bad dreams in which you are being chased, but you cannot move your legs.

The boat was stuck to the ocean like a fly to flypaper.

The Vikings blundered toward their oars, roaring in terror, pushing each other over in their panic.

Hiccup leaned as far as he could over

the side of the boat.

"WHAT...DO...YOU...WANT?"
Hiccup shouted at the Dreader in
Dragonese. "HOW...CAN...I...HELP
YOU?"

The tiny words were snatched by the
wind the moment they left
Hiccup's mouth.

DO YOU WANT?

Snatched, and tossed away, as the depression in the water deepened and gained and the wind screamed louder.

Hiccup HAD to get close to this dragon, so that he could speak to it. He just HAD to...

Thinking of nothing but getting near enough so his voice could be heard, Hiccup climbed the slippery dragon figurehead of the boat, his hands sliding on the cold wet wood, the wind tearing maniacally at his clothes and his hair.

"WHAT DO YOU WANT??" screamed Hiccup, louder still. "Please don't take our heads...or our blood, or our hearts...WHAT DO YOU WANT???"

And then right in front of Hiccup's terrified gaze, two enormous eyes rose to the surface, but did not break the water.

"AAAAAARRGGHHGHHHH!" shrieked Hiccup, as to his absolute horror, his hands slid on the wooden dragon's head. He couldn't keep his grip. He was going to fall into the sea, into the path of that dreadful creature.

He fell...

...and the back of his waistcoat caught on the edge of one of the figurehead's teeth, so that he hung there, dangling and scrabbling wildly in front of the advancing Dreader, like a fish on a hook.

Oh for Thor's sake, shrieked a voice in Hiccup's head. *I'm going to be the first to go...*

He braced himself for the Dreader's attack.

The mouth broke the water, and the creature screamed as if in pain. The wind from its inhaling mouth sucked the boat toward it, despite the Vikings desperately paddling with all the strength of their hungry limbs.

The inhaled scream of that
Dreader made the head ring from the
inside, as if it was a bell being rung by
Thor's hammer, but it seemed to Hiccup
like the weird, terrible scream contained
half-formed words in a very ancient
Dragonese indeed, and the words were:

361

Maybe that was what the words were, and maybe that wasn't—they were so unformed it was hard to say.

But on the final shrieking syllable the sucking-in ceased and the creature exhaled, and Hiccup's last thought was:

Here we go…The Dreader's going to use its power now…

And there was a truly earsplitting noise…A horrible choking yank at Hiccup's neck…

I'm going to die, thought Hiccup.

And everything went black.

8. DRAGONS ARE SELFISH—DON'T YOU KNOW THAT?

Now I'm afraid this doesn't seem a good moment to leave Hiccup, EITHER, does it, given that he's about to die?

But we just have to catch up with those cute and helpless dragon babies whom we left moments away from a messy death in the jaws of Fireworm.

This is all very inconvenient, but we can't leave the poor little things for one second longer.

You see the problem with storytelling? Sometimes so many things are going on at once you can't keep up with everything at the same time.

We had left Fireworm flying toward the open door of Hiccup's house, and as soon as she set eyes on those dragon babies, they would be EX-dragon babies, sure as fish eggs are fish eggs.

Toothless was watching from the roof
beam above, delighted that the
problem of the little pests was
going to be taken out of his
paws, because their
unbelievably
high-pitched
chirping was
giving him a
headache.

Papa is wonderful! Hic... whoops...

"Papa!
Papa! Papa!"
squeaked the
babies. "We love
you, Papa!"
Toothless
snorted disgustedly.

What was it with babies? Where was their sense of dragonhood? Dragons were selfish, and they didn't love anybody; didn't they know that yet?

And then the blue one shouted up, "Papa is wonderful!" and craned its neck so far backward as it leaned back to look up at him that it fell over—"Whoops!"— into Toothless's water bowl.

Oh fishhooks.

Something came over Toothless—he didn't know what. Toothless was more selfish than most dragons.

... splosh.

But whatever it was, it seemed Toothless couldn't let Fireworm eat the wretched little babies after all.

Quick as a diving falcon, he swooped down, plucked the blue one out of the water bowl with his mouth, the yellow one and the green one in each of his front paws, and carried them in a rain of goo and water up to the roof beam.

"B-b-be quiet!" he hissed at them fiercely. "Or you will DIE!"

"Oooh...Papa so brave," they all cooed.

"Oh f-f-f-fiddlesticks," sighed Toothless, his empty tummy grumbling even louder as he dived down again, panting, and perched on Stoick's chair back, trying to look unconcerned.

In the nick of time.

In through the open door swooped the lean, red panther body of Fireworm, a beautiful Monstrous Nightmare dragon, all gleaming muscles and glinting fangs. By some instinct, the squeaking from the roof

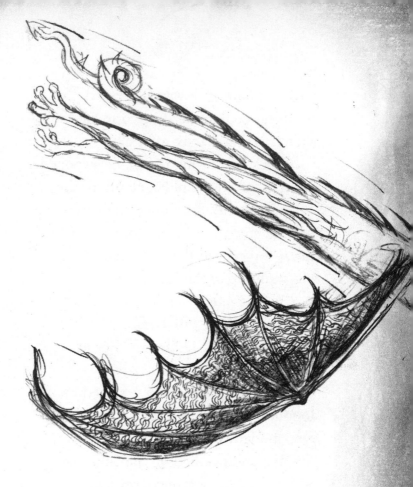

beam ceased instantly the moment she
entered. She glided slowly around the room,
like a gigantic, malevolent red bat sensing
drama, before landing on the hall floor and
sharpening her talons on the bright edge of
Stoick's axe.

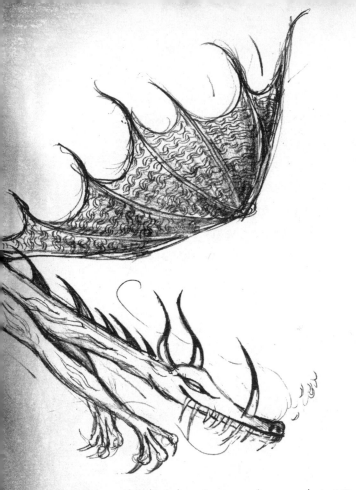

"What has been going on here?" she
hissed at Toothless, looking suspiciously
around the room, taking in Toothless's
blackened state, covered in charcoal and
goo. Her serpent eyes brightened as she
saw the lime-green slime dripped liberally

all over the place, and the spilled water bowl, and the thousands and thousands of pieces of smashed lime-green dragon egg.

"Babies?" she purred, licking her lips with her long forked tongue. "Delicious soggy gooey little dragon babies? Oh, how I love to wring their goggly little necks—the gooier the better! So, where are they, Toothless?"

So, Where are they,
. Toothless?

She pointed her pin-sharp front talon, long as a scimitar, right at Toothless's throat. "I know you would want to share..."

"T-t-toothless already ate them," said Toothless rudely, as careless as he could be.

It was very believable, for Toothless was the greediest little dragon on Berk, and he was covered head to toe in lime-green goo.

Quick as lightning, the talon came down. Luckily Toothless was quicker still, and jumped out of the way just as it plunged into the chair, practically carving it in half.

"Savage!" hissed Fireworm. "Greedy little mongrel!"

"You l-l-looking too fat, anyway, Fireworm!" jeered Toothless, sticking his forked tongue out at her.

Fireworm aimed a jet of flame at him, and again he dodged it. Nobody was better at dodging than Toothless.

Toothless thought quickly. He had to

get rid of her. "There's more of 'em, though," he said, pointing his wing to the door. "Out in the h-h-harbor..."

Fireworm's eyes lit up with greed.

"Watch your back, you inflated little flying toad," she warned Toothless nastily, as she flew swiftly out the door, to look for more delicious little dragon babies to eat.

Toothless heaved a sigh of relief.

She was gone.

But Fireworm had only just left, when…

BAM!

The first baby fell out of the hiding place.

It made no attempt to fly, just hit the floor with a sickening thud.

Screeching with alarm, terrified that it must have broken something, Toothless swooped down to it.

The baby gave Toothless an angelic smile. "I is *fine*!" it squeaked. "Don't worry!"

*Oh for Thor's sake…*Toothless

collapsed with relief, and...

BAM!

BAM!

Toothless jumped a foot in the air as the two other little babies slammed to the floor as well.

"We is fine *too*!" they squeaked, squealing with laughter at Toothless's alarm.

Poor Toothless had barely gotten over the shock when the little dragons shot off (at extraordinary speed, considering they couldn't fly yet and were waddling on little newborn feet) in three different directions, squealing: "We is hungry, Papa, HUNGRY!"

"What are you doing????" cried Toothless in alarm. "We have no food... Toothless promised he w-w-wouldn't make a mess...*What are you doing????*"

CHOMP! CHOMP! CHOMP! The little green one munched a huge chunk out of Stoick's chair leg. The little yellow one set fire to the chair, and the curtains, and

the cupboard. And—

"Hic...Whoops! Ow! ATISHOO!"

There was a mountainous clatter from
the pantry as the little blue one went
through it like a tiny dragon tornado,
sending pans and cauldrons flying in all
directions and bowling out the door.

"S-S-STOP!" cried poor Toothless,
trying to put out the fires and yelling at the
top of his voice. "STOP! NO CHEWING!
NO P-P-POOING! NO BURNING!
TOOTHLESS WILL BE IN SO MUCH
TROUBLE! STOP!!!!!"

To his passionate relief, and surprise,
the three little dragon babies shot wobbly
and obediently toward him. They came to
a halt underneath him, looking up at him

with
their
huge baby
dragon eyes,
innocently
questioning.

"Oh, thank Thor," panted Toothless, and he put on his most stern voice. "You m-m-must not burn anything...or eat anything...or make a mess...or T-t-toothless will be in BIG TROUBLE, understand?"

The three little dragons looked up at him.

"Papa is wonderful," said the little blue one.

"We promise we'll be good..." said the little yellow dragon.

But all three little dragons had their claws crossed behind their backs.

There was a slight pause.

And then the little blue one made a big pooey mess in the middle of the floor.

The smell was indescribable. How could something so small make such a huge stink?

And all three shrieked, "But we is HUNGRY!"

And off they dashed in three separate directions again, raking up the floors with their little dragon talons and setting fire to things. The little blue one was already in Stoick's bedroom attacking all the pillows, in case they contained food, and giving himself a coughing fit as he choked on the feathers.

Toothless was beside himself...

"AAAAGH!" he yelled. "STOP IT, YOU LITTLE H-H-HORRORS! STOP IT! TOOTHLESS'LL PUT BLACK MARKS ON ALL YOUR STAR CHARTS! TOOTHLESS'LL PUT YOU TO BED WITHOUT ANY DINNER! TOOTHLESS'LL...TOOTHLESS'LL~"

But whoever was the boss of those little dragons, it certainly wasn't Toothless. They took absolutely no notice whatsoever.

Gulp.
Toothless going to be in s-s-so much trouble.

9. BACK TO THE HOOLIGANS AND THE DREADER'S DREADFUL POWER

Now at least we know that the dragon babies are all right, even if they are destroying Hiccup's home. So we now go back to the Hooligans, who, to their indescribable terror, were just being attacked by the dread of the Dreader.

Oh, yes, and Hiccup was about to die, wasn't he?

I knew I'd forgotten something important.

Everything had gone black and warm and wet, and there was a horrible choking feeling around Hiccup's neck.

"AAAAAARGGHH!" gargled Hiccup. "AARRGH!"

For he thought he was about to lose his head, and maybe the warm-and-wetness was his own blood.

He was lifted upward, as if by the arms of Thor himself, and he imagined that perhaps he was dead already and being lifted up toward Valhalla?

The breath left his body with a sickening shock as he landed, sprawling and soaking wet, on some hard, flat surface.

His eyes had closed automatically, but now he opened them, slowly and stickily, for it was like they had been dipped in glue. His heart was palpitating with fear like a rabbit's, for he thought he was opening his eyes into the next world.

But the hard, flat surface he had landed on was in fact the wet wooden boards of the deck of *The Fat Penguin*, awash with some strange liquid substance much thicker than water.

Oh thank Thor.

He wasn't dead after all.

Yet.

Gasping, he looked upward through his gummy eyelids.

That choking feeling around his neck
must have been caused by Stoick hauling
him by the back of the waistcoat over the
edge of the boat. For Stoick was standing
over him, gasping in shock, covered in a
strange liquid blackness, his white eyes the
only color showing through.

All around the Vikings were screaming,
"MAKE FOR THE SHORE!" and
paddling like crazy, covered in this weird
shiny blackness and spattering little liquid

splats as they shoveled their way through the heaving sea.

The Hooligans did not stop to ask what had happened. They paddled like madmen for the shore, and it was only when they had landed all the boats in the harbor and staggered, dripping blackness, onto the beach, that they began to wonder what had gone on.

"Gobber..." said Stoick the Vast in a baffled, liquid sort of way, blowing bubbles through the goo that had gathered in his beard. "Gobber...what *is* this stuff? We seem to be alive, but this stuff is very..."

"*Smelly...*" Hiccup pointed out.

For now that the terror of the moment had passed, the smell crept up on them, a smell so appalling that the inside of the nostrils burned like acid. It was a smell so much worse than anything you've ever smelled

before. Imagine a skinful of skunks who had been exercising a lot without using deodorant. Imagine rotten eggs and stinking haddock and rotting corpses and Baggybum's socks after he's been playing bashyball for a couple of weeks, and you still haven't gotten there.

It was a smell so bad that it almost had a physical presence, as if a large, dead, wet walrus was hanging right in front of your nose.

"Stink dragon," panted Hiccup in wonder. "The Dreader is just a giant stink dragon."

"Hang on a second," roared Stoick furiously. "The Dreader's power, the power of the legend that has kept us hungry and eating nothing but limpets for the last six weeks, is *supposed* to be the power of removing people's heads! Or at the VERY LEAST it's meant to drive you mad, or suck out your blood until you're flat as a piece of paper…Are you telling me that this power the Sagas have been going on about for centuries is not any of these things, and it's just a *BAD SMELL*????"

"It looks like it," said Hiccup. "Legends do not always tell the truth. I guess if you're telling a Saga, a bad smell doesn't make such a good story."

"Well, you have to admit, it's not just a light odor," said Fishlegs. "This is the worst smell I have ever smelled in my entire life. I can feel one of my rashes coming on."

"I'LL NEVER BELIEVE A STORY AGAIN!" yelled Stoick, punching his fist in the air. "THIS IS AN OUTRAGE!"

For a moment it looked as if Stoick would explode.

Which would have been a messy business, what with all that yucky, smelly black stuff all around. But instead his shoulders began to shake. Stinky little droplets showered off him like smelly rain, as Stoick the Vast, O Hear His Name and Tremble, threw back his gooey black head and roared with laughter.

And then all the other Hooligans joined
in: HA! HA! HA! HA! HA! Laughing fit to
bust a gut, smelling to high heaven. No
one can laugh like a Hooligan can laugh,
great gusting belly laughs, even when those
bellies are empty.

"RIGHTO GUYS!" bellowed Stoick.
"Let's clean this stuff off, and go out and
catch ourselves some FISH!"

"Yes, but, Father," argued Hiccup. "The
Dreader is still out there, and he's still
gigantically enormous even if his dreadful
power IS only the power of stink—"

Stoick was suddenly serious again.

"Yes, you're right, Hiccup," he said, scratching his head and frowning. "This calls for another of my Clever and Intelligent Plans."

Hiccup sighed. It could take WEEKS while the wheels of Stoick's brain moved infinitely slowly to come up with something as ridiculous as the last Clever and Intelligent Plan. But Hiccup had more urgent problems.

For out of the corner of his eye he could see flames shooting upward on the hillside, right in the heart of the Hooligan village.

His father's house was on fire.

Toothless. Oh for Thor's sake, what had Toothless done now?

Everyone else jumped in the harbor, trying to scrub off the smelly stuff. SQUELCH! SQUELCH! SQUELCH! Dripping and reeking, Hiccup shot up the hill.

10. HAVING YOUR OWN PET IS A WONDERFUL THING, OF COURSE

SQUELCH! SQUELCH! SQUELCH!
Hiccup was holding his own nose to try to keep out the disgusting stench as he half staggered, half ran up the hill, his legs wide apart because the revolting Dreader-juice was sloshing around the inside of his trousers.

Bits of ferns and heather stuck to the stuff as he fell flat on his face, and staggered to his feet, and flung open the broken door of his father's home.

"AAAAAGHHHHHHHH!"

How could one small dragon cause so much devastation in so short a time? Furniture, crockery, weapons smashed, tables in flames, kitchenware scattered across the length of the room—it was as if a gang-load of fire-eating Berserks had been charging around the place on rhino-back.

"TOOOOOOTHLESSS!!!!!!!"
howled Hiccup, without really expecting
the little dragon to reply, but Toothless
swooped down from the rafters, in
passionate relief, only just stopping himself
from landing on his Master's sticky black
head in time.

Toothless was in tears.

"They w-w-won't do anything
T-t-toothless says!" wailed Toothless
desperately.

"What are you talking about?"
screamed Hiccup. "My father is going to
kill us, and then he'll throw you out, and
then he'll kill me again, and he was in
such a good mood—"

Toothless pointed a tragic wing
downward. "They did this! They
ch-ch-chewed everything, and they set
f-f-fire to everything, and they pooed
everywhere, and they w-w-wouldn't listen
to Toothless and it's...ALL...THEIR...
FAULT..."

Blinking through the stinking Dreader-goo, Hiccup looked down at his feet.

Three tiny little baby dragons were sitting in a row, one green, one yellow, one blue.

"Where did these dragons come from, Toothless?" asked Hiccup in a bewildered sort of way.

"Ah," Toothless looked guilty. "T-t-toothless found them...They hatched...from some eggs that t-t-turned up...Toothless was just out in the Open Ocean a couple of months ago, you see, and he found this little island, and these eggs were just l-l-lying there...Didn't seem to belong to anybody..."

"Toothless, I keep telling you not to steal dragon eggs; you never know what type of dragon they might be!" exploded Hiccup.

Now the little dragons turned into little hissing, spitting demons as they rushed to defend Toothless, who they thought was their father, against this horrible great big human who was being mean to him.

"Be nice to Papa!" spat the green one.

"Papa is wonderful!" said the yellow one.

And "Hic...Whoops...Atishoo!" said the blue one. And he opened up his little blue dragon mouth, and he inhaled with a little sucking noise, and then he exhaled, and out shot a little shower of black liquid.

It missed Hiccup's right foot by some distance.

The smell of it was extraordinary. How could something so tiny make a stench of such indescribable awfulness? A smell of rotting corpses, of stinking eggs, of dead, wet walrus hanging in front of your nose...

A-HA.

Suddenly everything fell into place.

Those eggs had just been lying there, had they? Somewhere out in the Open Ocean...

Hiccup bent down, scooped up the three little dragons in his arms, and shot off down the hill.

11. IT'S A MYSTERY

Down the hill, Hiccup ran, **SQUELCH! SQUELCH! SQUELCH!**, with the little dragons shrieking, and biting, and squealing, "Papa, save us! Papa, save us!" all the way down.

SQUELCH! SQUELCH! SQUELCH! Hiccup ran past the roaring, laughing Hooligans, still trying to scrub off the smell in the harbor.

Into his boat, *The Hopeful Puffin*, Hiccup jumped, and he wrapped the little dragons in his dripping waistcoat to confuse them and set the sails out to the dark shadow beyond the harbor.

He sailed out to where it was waiting, and then he shelved the oars, and drew out the little dragons, who bit him furiously.

"Papa, save us! Papa, save us!"

"HERE," said Hiccup. "This is your REAL Papa..."

And he dropped them one, two, over

the side. The third, the little blue one, had gotten a tight hold of Hiccup's trousers with his little jaws, and Hiccup had to work them free, and then he dropped him over the side as well, with a "Hic...Whoops... Atish—" SPLASH!

They swam instantly underwater, a flash of yellow, green, and blue, and the dark shadow shimmered under the water, and they were gone.

Hiccup could not see what was happening. No doubt explanations were going on under the water, but nothing could be heard.

There was silence.

Toothless was hovering over Hiccup's head. "What are you d-d-doing?" he squeaked, furious, outraged. "That D-d-dreader is out there...The Dreader will get them..."

"The Dreader is their...papa," explained Hiccup sternly. "Or parent, anyway."

"N-n-no!" exclaimed Toothless.

"Where did you find those eggs, Toothless? Those were the Dreader's eggs, and who could blame it if it came looking for its eggs? I have told you and told you, Toothless, not to go stealing eggs. And now you know why."

Toothless denied everything, swore he had come upon the eggs entirely by accident. But both he and Hiccup knew the truth of the matter.

And then far, far out in the bay, way, way in the distance, as it swam to the Open Ocean, the gigantic form of the Dreader LAUNCHED itself out of the water.

It was just a glimpse of this creature that never allowed itself to be seen by man, but what a magnificent sight it was, impossibly huge, a breathtaking green, not dreadful at all.

Hiccup caught his breath at the wonder of it. And was it Hiccup's imagination, or was the flipper raised in a sort of salute?

And was that three little specks diving
after it, squeaking joyously?

On the wind, the faint words in ancient
Dragonese:

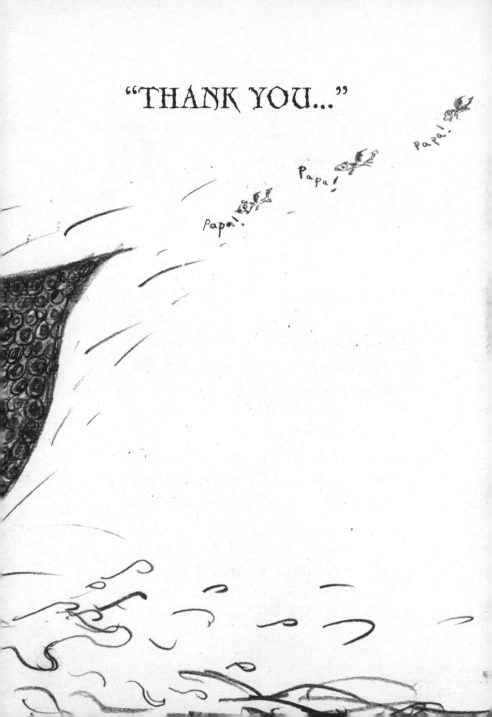

Toothless sniffed.

"Toothless'll miss them...They're smelly and n-n-naughty, but so *cute*...How can little dragon babies that cute grow up to be big, fat Dreaders?"

"I don't know, Toothless," said Hiccup shaking his head. "It's a mystery."

Hiccup sailed *The Hopeful Puffin* back to the harbor, and called out to the Hooligan Warriors, who had done the best they could to wash themselves, to say that the Dreader was gone.

"Excellent," boomed Stoick the Vast, rubbing his hands together, deeply relieved he didn't have to do any more of this brain work. "I **KNEW** that my Clever and

Intelligent Plan would work. And now I don't have to come up with another one! Watch and learn, my boy, watch and learn. It'll be a fish feast for supper then, guys!"

And off the Hooligan Warriors set, thinner and tireder and a great deal stinkier than normal, but as happy as anything at the thought of a limpet-free fish feast.

"And now, Toothless," said Hiccup, in his sternest voice, "hopefully my father will be in a better mood when he's gotten some food inside him, but still, you and I are going to tidy up what's left of that house before my father gets back."

Toothless thought for a second. He put his head on one side.

"Weeeeelll," said Toothless in the voice of a martyr. "This wasn't T-t-toothless's fault...None of this is Toothless's fault...Was all those dragon babies..."

"Toothless!" interrupted Hiccup in exasperation. "This was all your fault

entirely from start to finish! If you hadn't
stolen those Dreader eggs, the Dreader
wouldn't have followed us, and nobody
would have been hungry, and—"

Toothless ignored him in a lofty way.
"And T-t-toothless is tired...Got a
tummyache...W-w-want to go fishing..."

"I don't believe this," said Hiccup.

"B-b-but..." said Toothless,
considering the matter. "Toothless is not
a bad dragon like those dragon babies.
Toothless a GOOD, kind dragon, helpful,
thoughtful. Toothless sh-sh-shall help
the mean Master—this time..." he
said kindly. "Until Toothless's wings
start hurting."

~ DRAGON BEHAVIOR CHART ~

NAME: Toothless

BLACK MARK: ✗
STAR: ☆

	NO POOING	NO CHEWING	NO BURNING	NO STEALING	NO LYING
MONDAY	✗ ✗	✗ ✗	✗ ✗ ✗	✗ ✗	✗
TUESDAY	✗	✗ ✗ ✗ ✗	✗ ✗	✗ ✗	✗
WEDNESDAY	✗	✗ ✗ ✗ ✗	✗ ✗	✗ ✗	✗
THURSDAY	✗ ✗	✗ ✗ ✗ ✗	✗ ✗	✗ ✗	✗ ✗
FRIDAY		✗ ✗ ✗ ✗	✗	✗	✗ ✗
SATURDAY	✗ ✗ ✗	✗ ✗ ✗	✗ ✗	✗ ✗	✗ ✗
SUNDAY	✗	✗ ✗		✗ ✗	✗

EPILOGUE

Well, Toothless DID help Hiccup clear up that time (if you call "helping" flying around looking busy and tripping up Hiccup three times by accident), and he tried to be good for at least two weeks after that, before he forgot what it was like to look after dragon babies.

There was the most magnificent fish feast in the harbor that evening. Nobody even bothered to go home first. They just dumped the fish they'd caught on the rocks and built a fire right then and there and ate and ate until they were as full as fat walruses.

And then, oh, what dancing and celebrating there was under the stars that night!

Stoick was in such a good mood that he barely even noticed the remains of the destruction when he returned to the house. Even he, however, could not fail to notice the next morning the half-burned table and the remains of the door. But Hiccup said it was a passing Tigerbreath who had done it, and Stoick was so smug with pride and full of belly that he believed him.

As for the stinkiness, well, I'm afraid that such was the stench of the Dreader-juices. The entire Isle of Berk reeked like dead haddock for at least a month or so afterward.

But even that had its upside. The Uglithugs came creeping across in the dead of night on a deer-rustling raid on at least two occasions…and had to turn back when they came too close, on account of some of their younger Warriors feeling thoroughly ill at the smell.

Stoick never ate limpets again, and he never forgot his Clever and Intelligent Plan.

He had Fishlegs write him a small Saga called "The Day of the Dreader," which exaggerated everything terribly.

Fishlegs called the Saga "The True

Story of What Really
Happened on the Day of
the Dreader."

Fishlegs gave the
Dreader every single
terrible power he could
think of. He added at least
another foot to Stoick and
gave him a long, curling
mustache as well. According to the
Saga, Stoick not only had the brilliant
shield-bashing plan, he also fought the
Dreader in hand-to-hand combat and
circled the Isle of Berk twice while holding
on to one of the Dreader's tail fins.

So here we are at the beginning again.

Stories do not always tell the truth.

The bard gets carried away, legends get
added to and exaggerated, and so
gradually, gradually…the truth gets lost
along the way…

Stories do not always tell the truth.

Except, of course, for this one.

Don't miss Hiccup's next adventure!

How to Be a Pirate

1. SWORDFIGHTING AT SEA (BEGINNERS ONLY)

Thor was SERIOUSLY annoyed.

He had sent a mighty summer storm to claw up the seas around the bleak little Isle of Berk. A black wind was shrieking across the wild and angry ocean. Furious thunder boomed overhead. Lightning speared into the water.

Only a madman would think it was the kind of weather for a pleasant sail.

But, amazingly, there was *one* ship being hurled violently from wave to wave, the hungry ocean chewing at her sides, hoping to tip her over and swallow the souls aboard and grind their bones into sand.

The madman in charge of this

ship was Gobber the Belch. Gobber ran the Pirate Training Program on the Isle of Berk and this crazy voyage was, in fact, one of Gobber's lessons, Swordfighting at Sea (Beginners Only).

"OKAY, YOU DRIPPY LOT!" yelled Gobber, a six-and-a-half-foot hairy muscle-bound lunatic, with a beard like a ferret having a fit and biceps the size of your head. "PUT YOUR BACKS INTO IT, FOR THOR'S SAKE. YOU ARE NOT AN ICKLE PRETTY JELLYFISH. . . . HICCUP, YOU ARE ROWING LIKE AN EIGHT-YEAR-OLD. . . . THE FAT BIT OF THE OAR GOES IN THE WATER. . . . WE HAVEN'T GOT ALL YEAR TO GET THERE . . . ," etc. etc.

Hiccup Horrendous Haddock the Third gritted his teeth as a big wave came screaming over the side and hit him full in the face.

Hiccup is, in fact, the Hero of this story, although you would never have guessed this to look at him. He was on the small side and had the sort of face that was almost entirely unmemorable.

There were twelve other boys struggling with the oars of that ship, and practically all of them looked more like Viking Heroes than Hiccup did.

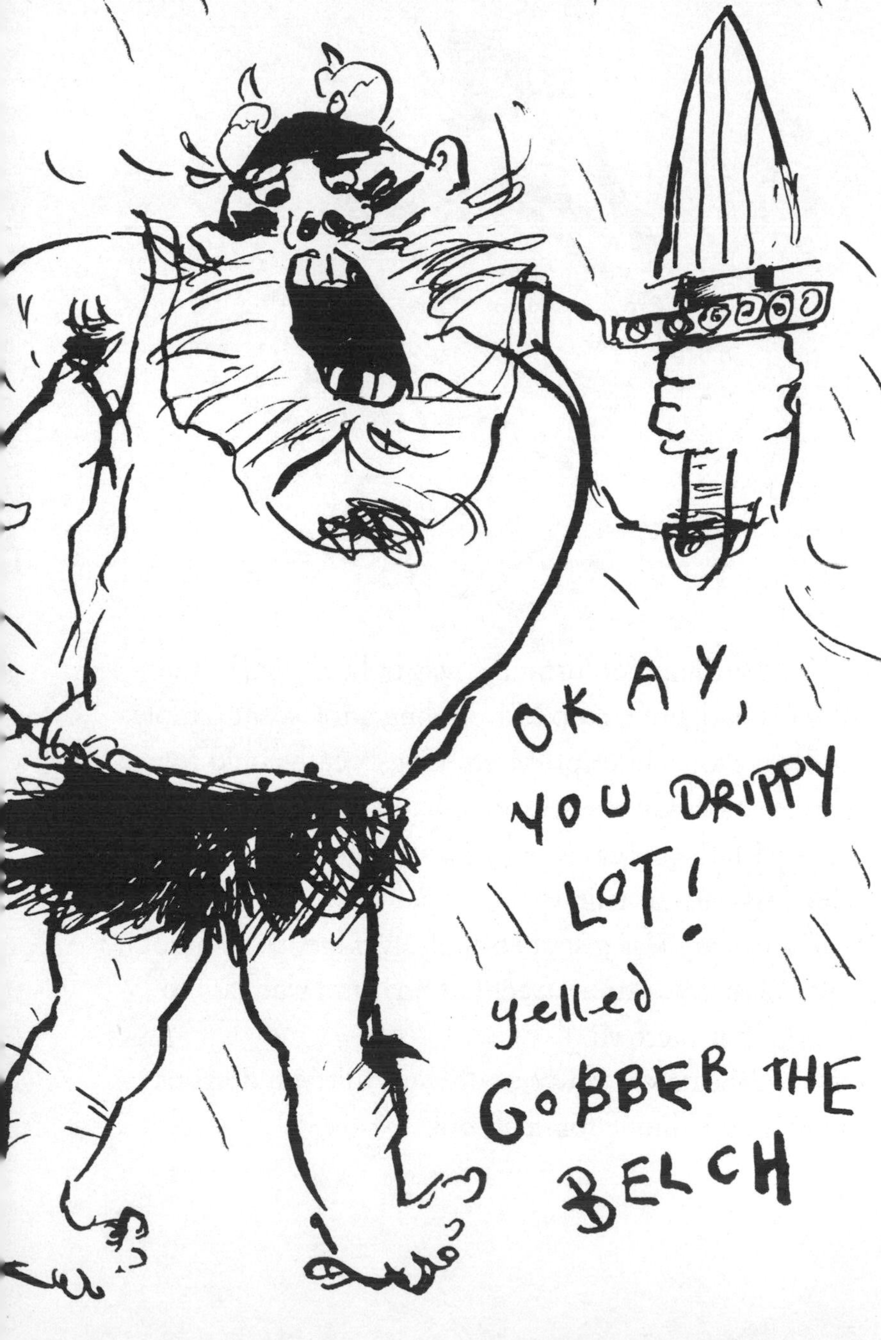
OKAY, YOU DRIPPY LOT!
yelled
GOBBER THE BELCH

Wartihog, for instance, was only eleven, but he already had a fine crop of bubbling adolescent pimples and a personal odor problem. Dogsbreath could row as hard as anybody else with one hand, while picking his nose with the other. Snotlout was a natural leader. Clueless had ear hair.

Hiccup was just absolutely average, the kind of unremarkable, skinny, freckled boy who was easy to overlook in a crowd.

Beneath the rowing benches, thirteen dragons were huddled, one for each boy.

The dragon belonging to Hiccup was much, much smaller than the others. His name was Toothless, an emerald green Common or Garden dragon with enormous eyes and a sulky expression.

He was whining to Hiccup in Dragonese.*

"These Vikings c-c-crazy. Toothless g-g-got salt in his wings. Toothless sitting in a big cold puddle. Toothless h-h-hungry. . . . F-F-FEED ME." He tugged at Hiccup's pants. "Toothless need f-f-food NOW."

a dragon's wings make a great umbrella...

---

* Dragonese was the native tongue of the dragons. I have translated it into English for the benefit of those readers whose Dragonese is a bit rusty. Only Hiccup could understand this fascinating language.

"I'm sorry, Toothless." Hiccup winced as the boat plunged maniacally downwards on the back of another monstrous wave. "But this is not a good moment. . . ."

"THOR ONLY KNOWS," yelled Gobber, "how you USELESS LOT got initiated into the tribe of the Hairy Hooligans . . . but you now face four tough years on the Pirate Training Program before you can truly call yourselves VIKINGS."

"Oh great," thought Hiccup gloomily.

"We will begin with the most important Viking Skill of all . . . SWORDFIGHTING AT SEA." Gobber grinned.

"The rules of Pirate Swordfighting are . . . THERE ARE NO RULES. In this lesson, biting, gouging, scratching and anything else particularly nasty all get you extra points. The first boy to call out 'I submit' shall be the loser."

"Or we all drown," muttered Hiccup, "whichever is the sooner."

"NOW," shouted Gobber. "I NOMINATE THE FIRST BOY AS DOGSBREATH THE DUHBRAIN. WHO'S GOING TO FIGHT HIM?"

Dogsbreath the Duhbrain grunted happily at the thought of spilling blood. Dogsbreath was a mindless thug of a boy with hairy knuckles that practically grazed the ground as he walked, and mean little eyes and a big ring in his flared nostrils made him look like a bristly boar with a bad character.

"Who shall fight Dogsbreath?" repeated Gobber the Belch.

Ten of the boys stuck their hands up with cries of *"Oooosirmesirpleasechoosemesir,"* wildly excited at the thought of being smooshed into a pulp by Dogsbreath the Duhbrain. This was predictable. That's what most Hooligans were like.

But what was more surprising was that HICCUP also leapt to his feet, shouting, "I nominate myself, Hiccup Horrendous Haddock the Third!"

This was unusual because while Hiccup was
the only son of Chief Stoick the Vast, he was not what
you might call "naturally sporty." He was nearly as bad
at Bashyball, Thugger and all the other violent Viking
games as his best friend Fishlegs.

And Fishlegs had a squint, a limp, numerous
allergies and no coordination whatsoever.

"What has got into you?" whispered Fishlegs.
"Sit down, you lunatic. . . . He'll murder you. . . ."

"Don't worry, Fishlegs," said Hiccup, "I know
what I'm doing here."

"Okay, HICCUP," boomed Gobber in surprise.
"Get up here, boy, and show us what you're made of."

"If I'm EVER going to be Chief of this Tribe,"
whispered Hiccup to Fishlegs, as he started taking off
his jacket and buckling on his sword, "I'm going to
have to be a Hero at something. . . ."

"Trust me," said Fishlegs, "THIS IS NOT
YOUR THING. . . . Clever ideas, yes. Talking to
dragons, yes. But one-to-one combat with a brute
like Dogsbreath? Absolutely NO, NO, NO."

Hiccup ignored him. "The Horrendous
Haddocks have always had a gift for swordfighting.
I reckon it's in the blood. . . . Look at my great-great-

grandfather, Grimbeard the Ghastly. Best
swordfighter EVER. . . ."

"Yes, but have YOU ever done any
swordfighting before?" asked Fishlegs.

"Well, no," admitted Hiccup, "but I've read
books on it. I know all the moves. . . . The Piercing
Lunge . . . The Destroyer's Defense . . . Grimbeard's
Grapple . . . And I've got this great new sword. . . ."

The sword was, indeed, an excellent one,
a Swiftpoint Scaremaker with go-faster stripes and
a handle shaped like a hammerhead shark.

"Besides," said Hiccup, "I'm never going to be
in actual danger. . . ."

The Pirates-in-Training practiced with wooden
cases on their swords. "Mollycoddling, we never did
that in MY DAY," was Gobber's opinion. However,
it DID mean the Hooligan Tribe ended up with more
live Pirates at the end of the Program.

Fishlegs sighed. "Okay, you madman. If you have
to do this . . . keep looking in his eyes . . . . keep your
sword up at all times . . . and say a big prayer to Thor
the Thunderer because you're going to need all the
help you can get. . . ."

Swiftpoint Scaremaker

Cressida Cowell grew up in London and on a small, uninhabited island off the west coast of Scotland, where she spent her time writing stories, fishing for things to eat, and exploring the island looking for dragons. She was convinced that there were dragons living on the island and has been fascinated by them ever since.

www.cressidacowell.co.uk